BS

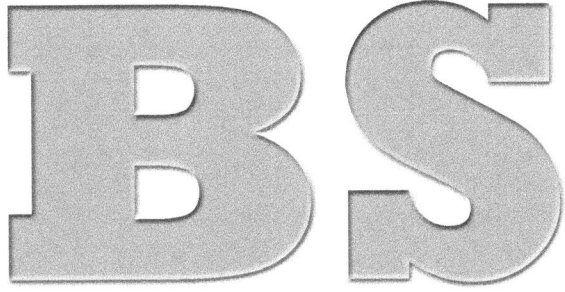

BS

a novel

by Steven L. Parker

Shawnee, Oklahoma

Red Dirt Press
1530 N. Harrison Street #143
Shawnee, Oklahoma 74804

Cover and interior design: Smythtype Design
Front cover photo (in part): Stock photo © Hlib Shabashnyi

ISBN 13: 978-0692470589

Contents

BS is dedicated to my brother, **JOHNNY RAY PARKER,** who was killed in Vietnam on March 21, 1969. Johnny never had the opportunity to write a novel, or to pursue the things his brothers and I have had the opportunity to pursue.

Author's Preface

While the characters in this novel are fictitious, I have known people who share the attitudes, determination, and grit of each one of the characters depicted in this book. The setting of *BS* is Southeastern Oklahoma; the beauty of this landscape and the personalities and mindsets of the people who inhabit this unique part of the state are difficult to capture in words. I have tried to present the magnificence, toughness, and resiliency of "Little Dixie," and I can only hope I have clearly conveyed these qualities to the reader so he/she will enjoy this novel.

—*Steven L. Parker*

ON THIS FIRST DAY OF JULY in the year of our Lord, 1975, two young men sat in a battered, honey mustard 1970 Ford Maverick and discussed their immediate future. The unremarkable building in front of them proclaimed the business it housed as Sam's Bar and Drive-in. Carhops in tight shorts and revealing blouses served beer to customers, soda pop (a rare order at Sam's unless used as a chaser) and sandwiches, usually hamburgers. A sign on the curve a half-mile away proclaimed, WELCOME TO CROW, FOUR THOUSAND FRIENDLY PEOPLE AND TEN OLD GROUCHES. The local Chamber of Commerce was certain the sign was one of the most innovative and original in the Sooner State.

The young men were drinking beer and planning their future in the farthest corner of the state bordered on the east by Arkansas and on the south by Texas. Oklahoma state loyalty was not a priority in this part of the Sooner state. All television programs seen by the local citizens originated from Texarkana, a city on the Arkansas-Texas line with citizens in both states, or from nearby Shreveport, Louisiana. Locals were much more likely to find their achievements recorded in the *Texarkana Gazette*, if at all, than in the *Daily Oklahoman* or the *Tulsa World*, both located far outside the Texarkana trade area.

Some of the citizens remembered a *Daily Oklahoman* reporter appearing when the courthouse collapsed in 1962, and for some manhunts of criminal perpetrators in the mountains nearby. Until Weyerhaeuser, the "tree growing company," moved into this part of the state, the forests were a true wilderness from which a knowledgeable local could remain out of the reach of the authorities until he grew tired of the chase. One such fugitive deserted the military during World War II and was never captured. He turned himself over to the authorities after the Vietnam War ended, creating a public relations dilemma for the U.S. Army who preferred he remain hidden, unknown and unseen. Should the deserter be pardoned, the rationale being the time he spent cowering and hiding in those rugged hills was sufficient time served away from society, or should the full weight of the U.S. government be brought to bear on the McCurtain County opposite of Sergeant York?

Instead of cowering and hiding, the former soldier had been living his life, oblivious to any search allegedly being held concerning his whereabouts. After two or three days, publicity in the state's two major newspapers fell off. The story died and no one in the area knew (or cared) what happened to the deserter. Now, the tree growing company brought their clear cutting philosophy to the former wilderness, expending its best efforts to change the formerly pristine Ouachita National Forest habitat to a man-made rural slum.

"I don't want to be Jesse James," Luther James, one of the two occupants—better known as "Bugger" to the citizenry of Crow—stated to his companion, Joe Burk. "I'm afraid we're gonna get caught, Brains."

Burk had told Bugger that his prison nickname was Brains, and it amazed him how Bugger not only believed it, but used the nickname unsparingly. He'd also just told Bugger that he was going to make him the second Jesse James. Burk hesitated, taking a swallow of the Budweiser the carhop brought before answering his companion. Burk had been a stellar performer on Crow's football, basketball and baseball teams in earlier years, but his luck soured after he left high school. He had just recently been released from the state penitentiary system but was still on parole, which meant the State of Oklahoma was still monitoring his activities. He was reporting regularly to a probation officer, and more irritating to Burk, was having to pay a $40 fee every month, money that could have been used to buy beer, chase girls, or do anything worthwhile—anything but pay it just to see the wimpy bureaucrat who sang the same song every month.

He watched the stocky, chesty carhop swish toward another car on the other side of the large parking lot outside Sam's Drive-in and Bar, and wondered momentarily if her come-on to him a few minutes before had been a part of the job, or if she was really interested. Having recently departed from the unfriendly confines of the Jess Dunn

Correctional Center in Taft, Oklahoma, he was certainly interested if she was, even if he was currently being serviced well in that area by Bugger's sister. Prison for the past five years had not afforded many opportunities for copulating with the opposite sex, and, contrary to public opinion, homosexuality did not appeal to many inmates incarcerated by the State of Oklahoma.

Burk glanced at Bugger, gauging the anxiety in his statement. He examined the neon lights in Sam's sign on the well-worn roof of the block building badly in need of paint, and thought nostalgically of the days he spent as a youth at this drive-in. He began buying beer at this hangout at the age of sixteen while still in high school, which was soundly condemned on Sunday mornings by regular churchgoers in Crow, even by the worshipers who had been drinking beer at Sam's the evening before. Burk personally believed that Crow had more than its share of churches, covering the gamut from Catholic to Baptist to Church of Christ, and every Holy Roller segment in existence.

Sam Stone, the proprietor of Sam's was a dark-haired, stocky, muscular man who appeared to treat all of his patrons with equal disdain. Burk had seen him pull a pistol from behind the bar, and fire several shots at Moses Wills, a Choctaw Indian, and a good friend of Burk's, who had elected to challenge Sam's authority to eject him from the night's activities at the bar. None of the shots hit Moses, either due to Moses's great speed or Sam's intentions. Sam refused to discuss his intentions, and Moses, after recovering from his initial resentment at being asked to leave, and being the target of gunshots, made the most of the event by comparing the zigzagging run to his open field runs on the gridiron while representing Crow High School some ten years before.

The Choctaw tribe was well represented in the area, having been forced into this part of Oklahoma by President Andrew Jackson via the Trail of Tears in the nineteenth century. The Choctaws had been a peaceful tribe of farmers living primarily in what is now the state of Mississippi. The black race was also well represented in this corner of the state, and Burk wondered fleetingly how many of the current Afro-Americans were descendants of the slaves who worked on the Choctaw cotton farms before the American Civil War. Given the plight of most of the Choctaw Indians in this corner of the state, he could not visualize "plantations" being owned by Choctaws, but he had read about Choctaws owning slaves and fighting for the Confederacy during the conflict more than one hundred years before. Stand Watie, a Confederate general who also happened to be a Cherokee Indian, was the last Confederate general to surrender. Burk read or had been told, he couldn't remember which, that a Choctaw Indian named Jones was the largest slave owner west of the Mississippi River before the Civil War. The tribe had certainly paid for picking the wrong side, Burk mused.

If you can maintain your perspective though, it all evens out, Burk reflected, thinking of Moses and the shooting incident. Despite the attempt to put a good face on it, this event crystallized for the patrons at Sam's that Sam meant business when he asked you to leave. Burk never had any trouble with Sam and considered him a friend. He did not know how soon this perception would be tested. Burk knew he was one of the few patrons of the bar who was aware that Sam had an invalid wife that he had cared for more than thirty years.

During his senior year in high school, Burk worked as an usher and bouncer for the local movie theater for two reasons. It allowed him to attend all the movies shown free, and it gave him a sense of power to be able to oust unruly patrons. He developed a habit of going to the Sunday night movie because most people in the churchgoing town of Crow attended Sunday night services, including the youth, and he did not want to attend those services, not even to meet girls. Burk did not want to think of himself as a hypocrite. He also knew the best movies were usually shown on Sunday in Crow, and he could savor the movie without relating to any of his peers if he went alone. His peers went to the Sunday matinee, and then spent the rest of the afternoon at the local Dairy Freeze, or cruising.

He had noted Sam Stone also was among the few Sunday night moviegoers in the small town, and that he was always alone. On one occasion when he and Sam exited the movie together, the bar owner acknowledged their acquaintance, offering the teenager a cigarette. When Burk declined, Sam grinned and said, "Staying in trainin'?"

"Naw, not really. I just don't want one now," Burk said, looking directly at the muscular bar owner. For reasons he did not understand, Burk felt comfortable talking to this man.

"I've noticed you here before on Sunday evenings. Is there a reason you don't go in the afternoon with the rest of the kids?" Stone asked.

Burk looked at him, shoved his hands in his pockets, and thought briefly of telling him to mind his own business. He had done it before with other adults who he didn't like, particularly when they wanted to pump him about his mother. Instead, he surprised himself by responding with uncharacteristic candor.

"Sunday night is my night to be alone. I like it," Burk said. He took his hands out of his pockets, entwined his fingers and pulled his arms tight.

Stone examined the boy carefully, then said, "It's my night to be alone too, but not totally by choice. My wife is an invalid who requires constant care, and this is the night her parents come to visit her." The duo stared at each other in silence, a silence which, however was not uncomfortable to either.

"What's the matter with her? How long has she been an invalid?" the boy asked.

It was Stone's turn to tell him it was none of his business, but he also responded uncharacteristically. "She got hurt in a car accident about seventeen years ago, probably about the time you were born. Look, I've got to go. I'll see you around."

Burk understood the exchange was over. Without Sam telling him so, Burk divined that the parents wanted to visit their daughter, preferring her husband not be present. Burk wondered if Sam had caused the accident that made his wife an invalid, but did not ask him. Burk never heard Sam mention his wife at the bar, finding few people knew about her. Sam sold beer and hamburgers, was always willing to be a listener, but talked very little, and never about himself.

When Burk first appeared at the drive-in/bar after the State of Oklahoma saw fit to release him, Sam treated him like he treated the traveling pipeline construction workers, or others from Crow who had to leave to make a living. Crow was primarily an agricultural and logging community, and did not afford many opportunities for sons and daughters of families who were not large landowners, nor holders of farms or timber interests.

Burk knew Sam was aware of his recent stay in the penal system, but also knew Sam would not dwell on his "misfortune" if he didn't. Burk had no remorse about being sent to prison for grand larceny. He felt that he suffered a stroke of bad luck when he was caught collecting the proceeds from a sale of Don Wells' calves that he and Steve Jones hauled to Ada to sell. Who would have thought that Wells kept such a close eye on the hundreds of cattle he owned and would have alerted sale barns one hundred or so miles away?

My God, the man had to be crazy, Burk reasoned. After all, Wells owned a local loan company, was elder of the Church of Christ, some kind of officer with the local Chamber of Commerce, and raised registered quarter horses. Who would have believed he arose at five a.m. every morning and drove to his various holdings, counting every cow and horse? It never occurred to Burk that the drive which Wells utilized to acquire his holdings also kept him awake day and night to keep those same holdings.

Burk was not lazy, but there had never been anyone to drive him, nor to even care much whether he existed or not. The energy level and drive of a man like Wells was difficult for Burk to understand. Wells' venom, however, regarding the thievery was something Burk could understand, even though he was the brunt of it. Burk, not being an acquirer of material things in his short life, nevertheless hated people who stole from him. He remembered the utter contempt he felt for another youngster who came from the same desperate straits as he did who'd stolen a shirt of his, and been dumb enough to wear it to school. Burk retrieved the shirt, and the thief received a valuable lesson.

After being caught with the hot cattle, Burk allowed himself to be persuaded to present his case to a jury of his peers by a young lawyer who thought he could make his reputation by winning an acquittal for the former star athlete. Burk realized too late that yesterday's exploits counted for very little when the facts and the law were against you. The young lawyer gained some trial experience, moved to Oklahoma City, and Burk got a prison sentence.

True to the region's reputation, he received a harsher sentence for cattle thievery than a killer on the same docket. He was sentenced to ten years with five years of the sentence suspended, while a killer who beat a motorist to death on the highway was fined $1,000, and given a thirty-day county jail sentence; the sentences were from the same jury panel. The killer did have to surrender the pool cue he used to kill the victim.

All of the locals claimed a man would get more time from a local jury for conviction of stealing a saddle or a cow than a killer would. Lynching was preferred for horse thieves, one wag proclaimed. Burk never saw or even heard of a lynching during his short life, but was aware that a prize horse or dog were more treasured by many of the local cattlemen than their wives or sweethearts or both—or so it seemed. He was also aware of a blacktop road with a long hill leading to Little River called "Nigger Hill" because a black man was allegedly lynched there in the nineteen twenties and his body buried in the hill. Burk thought of the many times he bicycled or walked over the body in the middle of Nigger Hill, and paused a moment. Times had changed for most of the rest of the world, but not for Southeastern Oklahoma, Burk mused.

Burk—never a quitter—intended to reacquaint himself with Wells again through Wells' loan company. Not that Burk intended to borrow money from Payday Loan Company, Wells' operation. He intended to rob it. Burk did not harbor malice toward Wells, but an added benefit to his planned heist would be to harm Wells. The old hypocrite had been vindictive at Burk's cattle theft trial, calling him and his accomplice "worthless scum." Wells had been particularly vindictive toward Steve Jones, because Jones worked for him. The wealthiest man in the area believed that a less than minimum wage job should keep people grateful to *him* for a lifetime.

Wells should have admired my efforts at becoming an entrepreneur, Burk thought. Wells had told Steve Jones, his theft companion, on an occasion when the youngster was working for him, that to acquire money, you could inherit it, borrow it, or steal it. Burk knew that Wells inherited his wealth. Given that neither Burk nor his accomplice would ever be likely to inherit anything of value, and that no one with a grain of sense would loan either of the cattle thieves any money of consequence, Burk thought it only fitting they follow Wells' advice, and steal.

Jones also considered their theft justified because he believed in Wells, and thought his advice sound. Jones should have known more about Wells' habits, Burk thought. Burk remembered that Jones actually believed that, if caught, Wells would request no charges be filed against him. He remembered Wells' tirade on the witness stand about how he'd given Jones a chance in life by hiring him, and then having his generosity rewarded by Jones stealing from him. Jones remembered the generosity otherwise; he left Wells employment because Wells deducted the cost of a shovel from his wages after the shovel handle broke when Jones was cleaning out a horse stall. Jones knew the shovel had endured many hours of use before it broke, and having to replace it with a new shovel appeared unfair to him. Nevertheless, he thought Wells would describe him, as he had in the hayfield, "the best doggone hay hand I ever had."

Wells learned at an early age that he could pay the locals almost nothing as long as he heaped praise on their efforts. "Doggone" was as close as he got to profanity, being a Church of Christ deacon and a God-fearing man. Burk had little time for sympathy for Jones, as Wells was equally efficient at heaping scorn on him during the trial.

"Mr. Wells, you are aware that Joe Burk, one of the defendants here, represented Crow High School on the gridiron, the basketball court, and the baseball field; that his lawyer believes the jury should consider those contributions in deciding his guilt, or in imposing sentence, are you not?" the prosecutor asked Wells when he was testifying.

"Objection!" the young lawyer, John Henry James, cried.

"Irrelevant and immaterial," the judge said. "Overruled. You may answer."

Wells looked at Burk slowly and then at the jury and said, "I don't know how many different kinds of balls he can play, but a thief is a thief. Christ forgave a thief on the cross, but it was after he repented. Neither of these low-lifes have repented, and my opinion is they should be hung."

"Objection! Objection!" shouted the young lawyer.

"Sustained. The jury will disregard this witness's last statement," the judge declared.

How in the hell do they do that? Burk wondered to himself. Besides, he would have been glad to repent, even to sackcloth and ashes. He wasn't given the chance, and both cattle thieves were treated equally, and received the same sentence.

Burk remembered his first meeting with the young lawyer who would attempt to keep him out of jail. His mother set up the meeting. Burk wasn't sure what his mother's relationship with John Henry James, Crow's newest lawyer was, but Burk recalled the lawyer was more interested in his mother's reaction to what he was telling his client than to Burk's recounting of his recent thefts. When she hugged him enthusiastically after he agreed to defend Burk and his companion, Burk wasn't certain he made the right decision. John Henry never discussed his fees with Burk, and his mother told him to not worry about it. Steve Jones complained bitterly about what he had to pay, before and after.

Ah, well, maybe she got something out of it, Burk reflected to himself while on the way to prison.

BURK READ A LOT in the prison library during his so-journ there and remembered a quote from a Frenchman who said, *behind every great fortune there lies a crime.* Burk now believed he had formulated the crime that would earn him his great fortune.

To many, Burk's "great fortune" would seem piddling and unworthy. Yet, to a thirty-year-old ex-convict who had been raised in a home with an alcoholic mother and no father, and in a home where Burk learned the term "Welfare Cadillac" did apply to them, and raised in a home where food became scarce at the end of the month while Mom was in an alcoholic daze as often as she could achieve it—to this man, his scheme was grandiose.

Burk grew to manhood in two and three room houses with no indoor plumbing, bathing in a washtub was the norm. No friends stayed overnight because he did not want anyone to see how he and his mother lived, and he was never sure whether his mother would be drunk or sober.

Burk's mother, Betty Burk, steadfastly refused to tell him about his parentage. His mother's main claim to fame in the area was that she, in an intoxicated state at the Broken Spoke Dance Club, a place for dancing, fighting, drinking and just general sinning on the Arkansas-Oklahoma state line, had pulled her skirt up to her waist when country singer Hank Thompson appeared there, and had him autograph her left inner part of her thigh, a scant half-inch from her panty line. *Ole' Betty was a hoot when she was tanked,* opined the spit and whittle group in Crow. Her son did not agree with this group. Between welfare stints, she worked as a waitress, fry cook, house cleaner, or baby sitter. Every job ended when she went on a vodka-induced binge, although some employers were willing to take a chance on her two or more times. When sober, she was a crackerjack worker with a pleasant smile, and a radiant light in her eyes that carried the fine sense of humor she liked to display when talking with nearly everyone. Yet, Burk remembered a sadness in his mother that she never shared with him. Indeed, mother and son really did not know each other well.

Burk had few male role models during his childhood as his mother did not appear to be that interested in the men who wanted to court her, but there were suitors, notwithstanding her seeming indifference. Burk thought he had cause for optimism, and hopes for a better life when Betty took a job in a local clothing store. She and the owner seemed to be destined for more than an employee-employer relationship. The job and the relationship ended when she went on an alcoholic binge. Burk remembered the binge occurred almost simultaneous with Sam Stone's being charged in the shooting death of one of his patrons. Sam claimed self defense, but speculation was rampant that he might have to serve time. Hopes were high in several congregations. His mother appeared depressed when told of Sam's plight, and began drinking again when the newspaper predicted a dismal future for the bar owner. The opinion—or hope—of the local newspaper was shown to be premature when the local judge dismissed all charges at the preliminary hearing. The Crow weekly newspaper thoroughly castigated the judge for applying what he believed to be the law of self-defense in the state. Burk remembered his mother sobered up for a while after that, and actually worked regularly at a local cafe. The relationship with the store owner ended. His mother—now dead—remained a mystery to her son. She died while he was serving his prison sentence.

Betty Burk remembered when she first saw Sam Stone. She was eighteen, lithe, brown-haired, intelligent—too much so for most of the males at Crow High School—and restless. Graduation just occurred for her and forty-four others, and she had no idea what she wanted to do with her life. Her parents made plans for her to attend either the women's college at Chickasha, USAO, or Oklahoma Baptist University in Shawnee. The schools in Norman and Stillwater were filled with veterans returning home from World War II and the party stories emanating from the local attendees—exaggerated to the nth degree—kept Betty's parents from entertaining any thought of their daughter going there. The state school at Durant was not much better, according to the locals. Sin was rampant on all campuses throughout the state, except those Christian schools that kept close rein on their students. This was the opinion of

Betty's parents, and Betty was aware this opinion would determine her immediate future.

Rebellion was not "in" at the time. Betty Burk was eager to see, experience, taste, and live this sinful existence at the big state university, but it appeared that it was not going to happen for her. Commiserating with Lois Johnson, one of her close female friends, who planned to attend Oklahoma State at Stillwater, Lois mentioned that Sam Stone, a fellow who was a few years older than the two girls, was rumored to have bet everything he saved of his military pay against the deed for a local tavern-grille just outside of town in an all-night poker game at a local motel, The Raven, and become the new owner of the establishment. Betty knew that Sam had been a devil-may-care teenager who may or may not have finished school before going into the army. And she was aware Sam received several medals for his World War II wartime service, but knew little else about him.

When her friend suggested they go to his establishment on a warm June evening, she went only out of a sense of adventure, and a desire to break free—at least momentarily—from the parental restraints which were binding her.

When she and Lois pulled into the parking lot of what was now known as Sam's Bar and Grille she was uncertain and apprehensive. Should she have ventured outside the protection of her parents? Even now her parents thought she and Lois were at a youth church meeting. What if someone saw her, and reported her to her parents? She was about to voice these thoughts to Lois, and ask her to leave when she saw the carhop advancing toward their car. Betty told Lois she would go with her to the parking area, but was not going inside under any circumstances. She recognized the carhop, Tina Evans, a girl who had been in her class through the eighth grade, but quit then, or shortly afterward. Betty hadn't known her during school, or seen her since their junior high days.

"Well, la-tee-dah, look who come to grace us with their presence," said Tina. "We don't serve water or milk here. What do ya'll want?" Tina smirked derisively. "Is church out tonight? Do you want me to call your parents for ya?"

Taken aback by the venom from the carhop, Lois shrunk back against the car seat and looked at Betty, who rose to the challenge.

"I won't tell your old man you're showing your tits for tips if you don't tell my old man about me being here. Bring us a pack of Pall Malls, and two Schiltz beers," Betty spouted, smiling brightly. Tina startled, taken slightly aback by the response, recovered quickly. She hadn't expected this kind of response from these do-gooders, but was equal to Betty's challenge.

"Hah! You're even greener than I thought if you think my old man gives a shit about me showing my tits. If he hadn't already seen them a hundred times, he'd be out here in this lot himself," Tina said. Looking at Betty, she snorted and emitted a sound which was either a laugh, or an insulting bray. "Too bad you ain't got any to show off, Miss Piss, I mean Miss Priss."

Lois looked at Betty, her face showing regret that she had intended to educate her less worldly friend. Betty, however, far from being offended, appeared to be enjoying herself.

"Look here, Tina-Tits, do we get what we ordered, or do we have to go in to complain to Sam about you not being nice to customers with money?" Betty asked mildly, still smiling brightly.

Tina, taken aback by Betty's attitude and words, looked at her as if she saw her for the first time. "I ought to whup your skinny ass right now, but I need this job," Tina whined. "Two Schlitz beers and a pack of Pall Malls coming up for the Queen of Sheba, and her maid." Tina made a mock curtsy, spat on the running board and walked off.

"That fat bitch, I ought to whip her butt, but it is your car. I guess I ought to let you have first crack at her," Betty stated, looking at Lois. She knew neither of them would be any match for Tina, but was enjoying Lois's discomfort. Seeing her friend's incredulous expression, she broke into laughter. Yes, this was beginning to be fun.

"Betty, are you crazy? That girl's likely to come back and whip up on you. She looks tough to me. Let's just get out of here. I don't really want a beer anyway," Lois said, a hopeful expression stamped onto her features. The sense of adventure had left her, and she was ready to retreat to safer environs.

"I don't think you have to worry about her. Look at what she sent, though," Betty said, watching two Hatfield-McCoy types advancing toward their car. Betty had seen Tina linger at a car on her way back to the bar, and the two occupants of the car were now approaching with a definite purpose.

The would-be Romeos split up in front of the vehicle, the shorter of the two advancing to her side of the car. Betty now had a good idea what Tina had been doing. The other advanced toward Lois. If they had not been so unattractive, Betty would have laughed out loud. Tina was good; she probably told her prospective suitor that she favored him over Long and Lanky on the other side. Her prospect smiled, revealing an absence of at least two front teeth.

"Look whut follered me home tonight, Pete," the short one called across the top of the car to his companion who was leaning on the car door, peering at Lois. Betty almost laughed. *Has this line ever worked anywhere on anybody*, she wondered, composing her features to register displeasure and anger.

"I don't keer. I like mine much better," Pete retorted, smiling, showing a full set of teeth, although somewhat tarnished. Lois looked at Betty apprehensively.

"Boys, I don't know what Tina told you, but we've got to get home to our husbands. You better just get along," Betty said, naively believing that the thought of husbands would quench the fire in the loins of the hunters.

"Hell, Betty, your ol' man cain't be taking very good keer of you, or you wouldn't be here. I can shore fix that. I can even give you recommendations." The gap-toothed smile appeared again. His use of her name confirmed that Tina sent the hopeful lovers. Betty began to feel some of the same apprehension which was written on Lois's face. Her mind was whirling, and she was ready to articulate a plea just to be left alone when another voice joined the dialogue.

"Joe, Pete, why don't you move along. These ladies don't want your company." The speaker was a muscular young man dressed in a short-sleeved shirt, and pressed khaki pants. Betty recognized Sam Stone. His eyes met hers, and locked. Betty forgot the would-be suitors. She felt that she and Sam were alone; while he also appeared to have forgotten why he was there. Joe brought them back to reality.

"Stone, git out of here. This ain't none of your business," Joe said. Sam had arrived at the passenger side of the car, and he and Joe were standing facing each other within two feet of Betty. Betty started to tell Sam they were leaving, and did not need his help. It was obvious to her that the situation was not going to get better. She saw Sam Stone's face turn stone cold. The blue eyes, which locked with hers just seconds before now locked with the gap-toothed would-be suitor, but conveyed a totally different message. It was a message that patrons came to know, and, for some, it was a message of dread which was violently unpleasant. Stone hadn't owned the bar long enough at this juncture for the hopeful hillbillies to be afraid.

"Everything that happens on this lot is my business. You boys need to leave. You can come back tomorrow night," Sam said, evenly.

"We ain't going, and you cain't...." Sam's palm thrust in the missing gap in Joe's teeth ended the sentence. Joe went backward, followed by Sam, who hit him in the forehead between the eyes, knocking him on his back in the gravel lot. Sam advanced to the fallen man, and placed a well-aimed kick to the jaw of Joe. Joe moaned, and raised his arms to shield his face. Sam kicked him in the ribs, and turned to face Pete who had come around the car.

"Do you want some of the same?" Sam asked Pete. Pete looked at Joe, who was moaning, and attempting to hold his jaw and ribs at the same time. Blood was pouring out of the gap in his mouth.

"Good God, Stone, you nearly killed him. Let me git

him, and we'll git out of here. All we wanted was a little pussy," Pete said, his voice ending on a pitiful note.

"Pick him up, and leave. Don't come back until you learn to behave," the bar owner said.

Betty was fascinated. This man had mutilated another man, but he appeared to be concerned about these two backwoods dolts remaining as his customers. Moreover, the two—or at least Pete, appeared to accept this as a normal routine. Joe was too busy moaning, and massaging his pained areas to be sensitive to what was happening.

"You kids better get back on your side of the tracks," Sam addressed Lois and Betty, turning his attention away from Pete and Joe who decided to seek their fun elsewhere. Betty bridled at the word "kids" but did not respond. She locked eyes with Sam again, but chose to say nothing. "Yes sir! We're goin'," Lois said, pushing the car starter with her foot. The car started and Sam stood back.

"Come back when you're older," Sam grinned, and pointed at Betty. Betty felt her face flush; she didn't know if it was anger or embarrassment. Who did this guy think he was anyway? So he beat up one hillbilly and intimidated another. So what? Betty and Sam were still looking at each other when Lois backed up and wheeled the car out of the parking lot.

Later, at Lois's home, Betty couldn't get him out of her mind. She pictured him standing with his hands on his hips, grinning foolishly at her. She felt she should be happy just being able to spend the night away from her parents. Her parents rarely let her stay away from home, and monitored all her activities. Her thoughts now were not what her Baptist parents would have approved. Although he called her "kid," his look hadn't called her a "kid." Moreover, she felt an unexpected rush of emotion when Sam pummeled the would-be lover. She intended to see Sam again; in fact, she intended to see him again tonight. She experienced another rush of emotion, akin to fear. Good Lord! Her parents would kill her. Lois's parents would kill her. For she intended to steal, or "borrow" the family car and travel back to Sam's and what? She didn't know how, but she was going to do it. She had noted the car was parked in the driveway, which slanted uphill. A little push, and the car would be in the street. The street ran downhill in one direction. With a little luck, she wouldn't even have to start the car until she was away from the house. She saw Lois put the car key on the coffee table, and assumed it would still be there.

Her luck held. The family decided to go to bed at ten p.m. in order to be fresh for church in the morning, which was one of the reasons Betty knew she had been allowed to spend the night in town. Both families attended the same church, and the Burks assumed one night away from the farm would not hurt Betty if she showed up for church on Sunday. Betty waited until Lois was asleep, then slipped quietly back into her clothes and out of the house. Borrowing the car worked as easily as she imagined it would to begin her great adventure.

Betty's heart pounded as she pulled back into the parking lot at Sam's Drive-in. Maybe this wasn't such a hot idea after all. What was she going to say to him? What if he laughed, and sent her packing again? She spotted Tina walking toward her, and bolstered her courage.

"Oh, shit, it's you again," Tina said. "What do you want? Do you want to see somebody else get beat up to save your precious honor?" Clearly, Tina was not overjoyed to see Betty back at the drive-in.

"Look, Tina, I know you don't like me, and I don't blame you. I want to see Sam Stone." Betty asked, feeling her face redden as she asked. "Would you ask him to come out?"

She had gone all the way from derision of the scantily clad carhop to obsequiousness. What was the matter with her?

"Good God, kid, he's married. Besides, he don't think of anything but how to make money out of this place. I know," Tina emphasized. "I know," she repeated with a smirk. Betty heard only the reference to herself as "kid."

"I'm no kid. Why does everyone here insist on calling me a kid." Seeing Tina's reaction, Betty changed course. "I'm sorry, Tina. If you don't want to tell him, I'll just leave," Betty said, looking as pitiful as she could.

"Hey, if you really want to see him that bad, I'll send him out. But you better order something. He certainly doesn't want to come out here empty-handed. You'd be better off just leaving, though," Tina suggested. She appeared sincere, which puzzled Betty. Why should this girl care what happened to her. Maybe she isn't as tough as she tries to pretend, Betty wondered.

"How about a Schlitz?" Betty inquired. "Is that O.K.?"

"So you're a big Schlitz drinker," Tina giggled. "One of Milwaukee's best for the valedictorian." She swung back into the drive-in, enjoying a private joke all the way back.

Betty thought, *Thanks for the promotion*, (she wasn't the valedictorian); *now what do I do if and when Sam Stone comes out here.* Minutes passed; it seemed like an eternity.

Betty kept her eyes trained forward. She did not want to meet Pete or Joe again, or any of their buddies. She saw a man who looked like one of her church's regulars, but he turned away, and she could not tell. *Does he really think I would tell*, she thought. *What would I say? When I was at Sam's Drive-in last Saturday night just before midnight, I saw Deacon Ellis attempting to get into Tina's pants. Yeah, well what were you doing there? I've really got to quit having these conversations with myself.* When she looked up, Sam Stone was inches away from her, looking into the car.

"What are you doin' back here? Lookin' for your boy-friend? I don't think he'll be back tonight," Sam said, lean-ing forward on the car window. His tone was mocking, and Betty noted he was empty handed.

I must be a fool, she thought, *to have come back out here and be humiliated by someone I don't even know.*

Without responding to his sarcasm, she leaned for-ward to step on the starter and leave. Sam, noticing her ac-tion, tried to pull back from the window, and bumped his head when he raised up.

"Oh, sheeit! That hurts," he exclaimed, wincing and holding his head.

Involuntarily, Betty giggled. "I'm so sorry. Is the big, bad bar owner going to cry," Betty mocked, conjuring up a look of maternal concern.

"Ha! You're real cute," Sam said, looking at her fully. Then, as if he really noticed her for the first time, he said, "By God, you are real cute. Yeh, Betty Burk, you are cute. In fact, you are beautiful." Sam concluded by looking deeply into her face, ferreting out emotions unfamiliar to Betty. She could not think of a response, but knew she did not want to leave and took her foot off the starter.

"How did you know my name?" she heard herself ask before being aware she was speaking. God, what a dumb thing to say. She felt her face begin to redden again. Sam laughed aloud, enjoying her discomfort.

"Tina told me Betty Burk, the queen of Sheba, demanded my presence at her car window," Sam said. "Besides, I remember when you were a cute little girl, and we attended the same school, although you're a lot younger than I am."

"I may be younger, but I'm not a *KID*, like you called me earlier," Betty said indignantly.

Sam looked her over with an appraiser's eye, and their eyes met again. For a moment, neither spoke. "No, I can see you aren't. I promise you I won't make that mistake again," he said, then raised his head as the lights of the drive-in began to blink.

"What's going on?"Betty asked, noting Sam's interest being diverted.

"Nothing. The lights just mean 'last call' before I close this place. You almost didn't catch me," Sam said. He looked back toward the building and saw Tina looking at him inquiringly. He appeared to hesitate, then turned his attention back to Betty, who was preparing to deny she was trying to *catch* him.

"Would you like to stay a while? It won't take me long to close up. You can drive around back and go in the back door. I have a room in the back where I sleep at times. I'll meet you there," Sam stated the last confidently as if the meeting were already arranged.

Betty hesitated. The night was slipping away, and

she was straying further from her parents' teaching than she had ever done. She looked up at Sam, who was looking at her in a gentle way, a look of tenderness on his face that was surprising to her. Particularly after the violence she had seen him perpetrate just hours before. She couldn't refuse.

This was the beginning of the best two months of Betty Burk's life, or so she told her friend, Tina Evans, before she died. For she and the girl from the wrong side of the tracks who she thought was a hardened floozy and just a carhop, became acquaintances, and then friends when she began seeing Sam. Betty arrived back at Lois's home on that first occasion before anyone awoke, and no one knew the car had been moved. She was to use this ruse twice more, and every other ruse she could manufacture to spend time with Sam that summer. The two laughed together, played together, floating on the raft on the river in the most wooded of areas, not always clothed in more than God's good flesh, and they passionately made love together. Betty was certain that no one before in human history could ever have loved as completely as she and Sam.

Sam assured her that he was going to get a divorce from the woman he married before going off to war, claiming the marriage was a hurry-up event which he consented to because he felt he would not come back from the fighting. Betty believed him. She knew Gail, Sam's wife by reputation only, and could not imagine Sam married to her. Gail's father was a wealthy farmer who also loaned money to certain selected borrowers. Betty wondered if Sam was one of those borrowers, particularly after he renovated the business, added more lighting, and hired another carhop. Sam never discussed his business with Betty, and she didn't care. He was much better educated than most locals knew, and Sam wanted to keep it that way. A well read bartender didn't improve beer sales, and certainly book reading was not an asset when forcing a redneck to leave the premises.

Near the end of this idyllic time in her life, the fates conspired to end the lovers' dreams. First, Betty guessed she was pregnant. Sam said he was going to divorce Gail, and had even told her when he planned to tell Gail about Betty, and his desire for divorce. Gail's family was planning a family reunion in Grayson County, Texas, and Sam was going. He planned to leave the wife he did not love after the reunion.

Before leaving, Sam drank a six-pack of beer. Some who thought they knew Sam said it was excessive; others claimed it was not unusual for him to consume beer before traveling.

While driving to the reunion, Gail and Sam drove in silence. More like Greyhound bus seat companions than a married couple who knew much about the other. In any event, Sam did not see the horse come out of the bar ditch of the Red River. The horse came through the windshield on Gail's side of the car, landing on her. She was taken to Texarkana, Texas, where she remained in the hospital for six weeks. Her life was spared, but she was to be confined to a wheelchair for the rest of her life, a quadriplegic. In those days of open range, the horse owner also sued Sam for destruction of his best roping horse. Sam reached a settlement with the horse's owner, and made a settlement with himself—to take care of Gail for the rest of her life. There would be no Sam and Betty. There would be no divorce. When he told Betty, she did not plead or beg. She did not tell him she was pregnant.

When the time came for Betty to be sent to the Oklahoma College for Women in Chickasha, a decision made by her father, Betty thought the honorable thing to do was to tell her parents she was pregnant. After all, she was not going to be able to hide her condition, and abortion did not cross the mind of the sheltered, naive farm girl. She was not aware of how totally imbued her Daddy was in the teachings of the Bible until she told him and her mother about the grandchild they were going to have.

Betty knew there would be consequences, but even she could not believe the reaction by her God-fearing father. The initial storm was nothing compared to the gale she wrought when she refused to tell them the name of the father of the soon to be born child. Daddy felt the scandal could be handled by a quick marriage to a family friend's son in Enid. When it was obvious that his headstrong, sinning daughter was not going to do what he wanted, he thundered that he had no choice but to invoke the Biblical sanctions found in Deuteronomy.

"The Bible says, a whore shall be stoned to death when she has plied her whoring trade in her father's house," Daddy had proclaimed a scant half-inch from his daughter's frightened face.

This puzzled Betty, since Sam had never been to the Burk farm, much less engaged in sex with her *in her father's house*. Besides, Betty did not buy into the "whore" characterization at all. Sam was her first and only lover. Betty had been whipped, and humiliated by her father on many occasions for many sins, but had never seen his face so fiery red and judgmental. She tried to speak.

"Daddy, we never did...." she began.

"Shut up, and git out. A bastard shall not enter into the congregation of the Lord, not even into the tenth generation. I won't have a bastard in my house. GIT OUT, GIT OUT, GIT OUT," Betty's father roared.

After reading the part again to his daughter where she should be stoned to death for her transgressions, he packed her clothing, shoes, and anything that indicated she had ever been a part of the Burk home, threw them in Piggly Wiggly bags and tossed them to the porch, and told her to depart, and not return. In the years that followed, every time Betty remembered her former life as the daughter of a good Baptist farmer, she remembered the red face of her father. She had little use for God-fearing farmers during the remainder of her short life.

Betty's mother, saddened by the event, did not defy her husband's edict. He had rescued her from a sharecropper's home where she shared her misfortunes with ten other children. Birth control was almost unknown in the early part of the twentieth century, particularly in Little Dixie, as the Southeastern part of the state was known. Besides, more children meant more cotton choppers or cotton pickers for the sharecroppers. Betty's mother, having escaped that life, did not intend to return to it by defying her husband. She, indeed, had been secretly grateful that, after Betty was born, she became ill and was told she could bear no more children. Her husband, being the God fearing Baptist farmer, could not banish her from his home, but he could have nothing further to do with a woman who was not a producer. Had she been one of his cows, she would have gone to the sale barn. There was no help from that quarter for Betty, nor would there ever be. Grandchildren were secondary to survival for Betty's mother.

Betty hitchhiked to town, got Tina Evans to help her move her belongings into Tina's small apartment, and left her parents' home forever. Tina was apprehensive at first, but knew Betty had no other alternative. Roy Burk's fellow church members were not going to help his whoring daughter. She and Tina got drunk the first weekend. Betty stayed with her to celebrate her freedom. Betty was rarely sober for any appreciable period of time afterward. Joe Burk was born seven months after her removal from her parents home. His birth was in the small apartment, and was attended by a midwife, and Tina.

Sam heard about the birth, and attempted to see Betty. Tina met him at the door of the upstairs apartment, and told him Betty would not see him. Sam pushed her aside, and went into the bedroom where Betty and the child were; Tina was now sleeping on the couch of the small apartment. Space was limited, and privacy non-existent. Betty and Tina had no secrets; each knew the truth about their sex lives. Thus, the conversation between Betty and Sam was certainly surprising to Tina.

"What are you doing here, you bozo?" Betty said, snarling at Sam. I'm not putting out for nobody now, and certainly not you."

Sam, taken aback, looked at Tina as if to ask what happened to the Betty Burk he knew. Betty hit him with another salvo.

"If you came to claim credit for this," she said, holding the newborn baby at arms' length, "you can forget it. I've had plenty of others since you, and this baby is a preemie. It couldn't be yours. So why don't you get your ass out of here and leave me alone. And don't be bothering my son."

Sam's face turned red. His fists clenched. The bar owner looked at Tina, who had a confused, puzzled countenance. He looked as if he were going to say something to Tina, changed his mind and strode back out of the apartment. Tina looked at the open door, then back to Betty. She was incredulous at what just happened.

"Girl, are you crazy? That man wants to take care of that child. And I KNOW you haven't been fucking anybody since you've been here. That boy is his child," Tina said, her hands on her hips, daring Betty to challenge her. Looking at Betty's face, which changed to utter woe, Tina changed course.

"Queenie, how do you think you are going to keep him from finding out that's his boy?" Tina said. "I know it, and you and Sam may have believed no one knew ya'll were foolin' around, but don't count on it. I've had some regulars asking about it."

"But you didn't tell. I know you, and now he doesn't know what to believe. Leave it alone, Tina, and quit calling me Queenie. You know I hate that," Betty said, ending with a smile. Tina smiled back, thinking, if you only knew how beautiful you are when you turn that smile on. The two had become true friends, particularly after Tina witnessed Betty's rejection by her former "friends" after the pregnancy became obvious, and the news spread about her father ousting her.

"Don't worry. Joe and I'll make it. Give me a drink of that Crown Royal your last boyfriend left. I need a pick-up," Betty said, grinning.

"How'd you know he left Crown...," Tina started, then thought about the living arrangements. "We really are going to get a bigger place." Both girls laughed. Tina never mentioned Sam's paternity again.

Burk's impoverished childhood was vividly stamped in his psyche when, at military basic training at Fort Jackson, South Carolina, he heard a Jewish recruit from New Jersey named Weinstein or some similar name complain to another squad leader about those *damn Southern rednecks*. "Those sons-a-bitches never had anything to flush. Trying to keep a latrine clean with bastards who never flush makes my job as a flush/leader since I have to go flush the toilets after checking them," Weinstein said to his fellow squad leaders, who guffawed, including Burk.

Although Burk joined in the laughter, he disliked the Yankee Jew for ridiculing him and others. Unaware he had offended Burk, Weinstein attempted to befriend him, particularly after Burk became a star player on the regimental football team. Burk rebuffed his overtures.

Besides the offensive remark, the Jews got too many holidays in the service, anyway, Burk thought. They got to celebrate all of the Christian holidays, plus all of the Jewish holidays. The only Jewish family in Crow, insofar as Burk knew, was a family with a cut-rate dry goods store. The clothes were cheap there, and it was where he was usually taken by his mother for school clothes.

Burk knew his mother was a good student at Crow High School, graduating in the very top of her class. Forty-five students graduated with her, and he had found a yellow, aged *Crow Gazette* story which carried her picture and four others as the top five percent. Betty Burk joked during her short life that she was the number five slot out of the forty-five machine. During periods of sobriety, she encouraged him in his school work.

Burk knew also his mother's parents owned a farm near the Red River, approximately three miles from the Oklahoma-Texas line. Burk knew that her father (Burk's grandfather), had been a deacon in Wildwood Baptist Church, and forced her out of the home when she became pregnant, and that Betty would not tell him who the father was. He learned that his grandfather caused Betty's name to be stricken from Wildwood Baptist rolls, and forbade his grandmother ever to speak to Betty again. Local Baptists viewed themselves as good Christians, and tried to keep out those who might sully their church—unless they had ample money to contribute to building funds and other such important events. Insofar as Burk knew, his mother never had contact with her family after she left home at the age of eighteen while pregnant, unwed, and unemployed.

His only memory of his grandfather, and he wasn't sure if he remembered or dreamed it—was an event where he and his mother got out of a car, and approached a farmer plowing in a field. He thought he remembered his mother calling the man in overalls and a welding cap "Daddy." He was certain he remembered the man pointing at the car, and telling them to get back in it, and off his land. He faintly seemed to remember his mother crying, and the difficulty he had negotiating the furrows in the rich black earth with his short legs as they left the farmer standing in the field. If the event had not been a dream, it was the only memory he had of either grandparent.

The grandparents were killed in a two-car accident in Shawnee, Oklahoma while visiting Oklahoma Baptist University (OBU) where they had just signed a Last Will and

Testament devising and bequeathing most of their worldly goods to OBU, enabling the university to carry on God's
work. Their joint will provided that their daughter received
$5.00 if she didn't contest the will, and nothing if she did.

Betty Burk took her $5.00 from the lawyer, who was
named in the will as the executor, and who was also a deacon in the Wildwood Baptist Church. She bought herself a
fifth of Jack Daniels whiskey, and partied until the fifth was
gone. The Wildwood church also received a healthy bequest,
which was used to buy new pew cushions and renovate
their sanctuary. The thirty-five to forty member congregation was much more comfortable on Sundays and Wednes-
days when their exhorter told them they were part of the
one hundred and forty-four thousand who were destined
to go to Heaven, and that all others were destined for Hell,
particularly those congregations which simply sprinkled
instead of dunking during baptism. He told them to look it
up in Revelations if they didn't believe him.

Joe Burk knew Betty Burk was rarely sober for more
than two months in a row after the death of her parents.
Burk promised himself that if he ever became respectable,
he would be a Baptist or Church of Christ member. He noted that all of the power and money in Crow seemed to be
lodged securely in churchgoers from those two congregations. There was one Presbyterian family with money, but
Burk considered that to be an anomaly.

Betty Burk remembered well the trip she made to her
parents' farm when Joe was two years old. She was working
at the E-Z Fold Chair factory, a Georgia company that rented a former cotton warehouse to manufacture cheap picnic
furniture to be sold across the South. Betty had taken a job

as a seamstress. With her pay and Tina's pay from Sam's, the two women moved into a small, comfortable house. Life was much better for the outcast from the Wildwood Baptist Church. An incident, which involved her two-year old son made her think of her father. Joe was standing near Tina and one of her male admirers on their small front porch when the suitor, intending to step between Tina and the edge of the porch, stepped into the small boy, knocking him backward off the porch. The boy, instead of falling backward to the ground, flipped and landed on his feet.

"Migod! Did you see that?" the boy friend said. "That kid could be an acrobat."

Betty appeared just as the courter finished his sentence, and said, "Well, his grandfather could clear a good sized horse. Maybe he takes after him," Betty remembered an occasion when her father was trying to sell a horse, and entered into an agreement with the prospective buyer that if he could jump the horse, the man would pay more. The buyer, looking at the horse, and considering further it was likely the horse would move when he saw someone running at him, thought he had a safe bet-agreement. Her father refused to call it a bet; it would be adverse to his Baptist beliefs. He called it a bargaining tool. Those who knew him well also knew none of his horses spooked when he ran at them. Jumping on or over them was not unusual on the Burk farm. The prospective buyer was entertained by an athletic feat, which cost him more than he intended to pay for the horse, and he was the butt of some ribald remarks when he told the story of the jumping farmer at the Crow sale barn the following week. There were others who had had to pay extra at Burk's, but admitting it to the latest buyer was not in their plans.

After the porch incident, Betty began thinking about all the things she left behind on her father's farm. Perhaps it wasn't fair to her son that he never know his grandfather. Or that the grandfather never got to admire the obvious physical skills of his grandson. Maybe the hateful words spoken to her almost three years before were retractable. She needed to see for herself. When she told Tina, she was puzzled by Tina's efforts to dissuade her from seeing her father. Tina had a lifetime of experience with God fearing farmers, and was certain Betty's father would not have changed in two or three or ten years. Tina could not sway Betty, though; she intended to mend the fences, and unite the father with his grandson. Tina met the grandfather in a chance meeting in Crow, and his castigation of her on the public sidewalk as the other whore convinced Tina that no good could come of any attempt by Betty to reunite the family.

As she drove toward her former home, Betty saw her father plowing a field north of the homestead. She stopped, picked up Joe, climbed over the fence and walked across the freshly plowed field toward her father. The black bottom land felt good to her, and she was glad she came—but not for long. Her father saw her coming and killed the tractor, a new model attesting to his success as a good farmer.

"What are you doing here, you Jezebel. I told you years ago to git off my property, and stay off. I meant it then, and I mean it now. Git out, and stay out," Roy Burk, red-faced and angry, shouted at the small woman and the child who was having a hard time staying upright in the soft black earth.

"Daddy, this is your grand...," Betty began.

"That little bastard isn't any kin of mine. Git him

and yourself off my property before anybody sees you here, and don't come back." The father/grandfather's face was contorted and red with fury. Betty withered before the venom. She took Joe's hand and half-dragged, half-led the boy out of the plowed field. Tears streaming down her face made walking over the plowed field difficult, and she fell. Then anger and resentment took over. Vowing she would not give that hateful Baptist, sanctimonious son-of-a bitch the satisfaction of seeing her cry, or fall again, she picked herself up, looked at the contorted features of her father, and walked out of the plowed field with as much dignity as she could summon. She never again tried to contact either of her parents.

Steven Parker

BURK HAD BEEN A MEMBER of the Oklahoma National-al Guard, and served only six months active duty, eliciting contempt from both those who fought in the Vietnam War, and those who ran away to not fight in Vietnam. He was, as he said, when asked, a one hundred eighty day wonder warrior. He had not joined the National Guard to escape being sent to Vietnam, nor to fight in any war; he joined during his junior year in high school because it meant he got some spending money every three months when he got his National Guard check. *I'll pay you when I get my Guard check* was an utterance familiar to any Crow merchant willing to extend credit to Burk. To his credit, Burk usually lived up to those promises.

This former National Guardsman thought his planned robbery was an enormous undertaking, which would be the first step in a bright future. He could not know his planned robbery would take a fateful turn, which in terms of dollars taken, would be much better than he had ever dreamed.

Burk intended to rob Payday Loan on the first day of the month. Having seen his mother and her acquaintances make trips to Payday Loan immediately before their welfare checks came in, Burk reasoned that the loan company would have a larger than usual stock of cash on hand on the first business day of the month to take care of the patrons who were short of cash before their checks came in, and also to cash the welfare checks of those who came in to make payments on loans already obtained.

Burk knew, at two hundred forty percent, some of those loans never got paid; the loan company renewed the loan, gave the borrower a small amount of cash, and waited until the first of the next month to start the cycle over again. Burk's mother borrowed $200 before he went to prison five years ago, and when she died while he was in prison, Wells came to repossess the television she pledged as collateral. She still owed $200 plus interest.

Legislators bemoaned the practices of these loan sharks when speaking in poor neighborhoods, or to ACLU types, but gladly accepted the campaign contributions of Wells and his competitors, reasoning that poor people had to have a place to borrow money and these high interest lenders were, indeed, providing a needed social service. The term, loan shark was not a useful phrase when one was seeking campaign funds.

Sorting through his mother's meager belongings after her funeral during the only time he was able to leave the prison during *his* period of incarceration, Burk found what he considered to be an odd memento. It was a picture of a

young Sam Stone. The inscription on the back had been ru-
ined by water, tears, or some other liquid. Sam had apparently written something to Betty Burk many years earlier,
but now it could not be deciphered. Burk wanted to ask Sam
about the picture, but never found the right opportunity to
approach him. He kept the picture in his wallet, although
on the only occasion when he was asked to explain why he
was keeping a picture of the local bar owner, he stuttered
and could not explain why. He simply made sure no one else
went through his wallet again.

On several occasions, when he had an opportunity
to look into the stands at various sporting events in which
he was playing, he saw Sam Stone watching the games. But
there were also many others who had probably seen a ma-
jority of the games he played in high school. But there were
events that made him wonder about his mother and Sam
Stone.

On one occasion, when he suffered a mild concussion after being tackled near the sideline, Sam Stone came
out of the stands and offered to take him to the hospital.
Burk and the coach declined. His mother's reaction when
he told her later surprised him. She got angry, called Sam
"a duty bound son-of-a-bitch," and swore that she would see
that "damn bar owner" would never take her son anywhere.
It was totally uncharacteristic of his mother, but she refused
any further discussion about the subject.

At times, Burk hated his mother for her alcoholism,
and the life he had to lead because of her. He spent as much
time parenting her as she had parenting him, he reflected.
After her death, he determined that he would simply try
to forget her; hating a dead person was unproductive. Burk

knew, however, that he would forever resent her for her re-
fusal to divulge the name of his father.

Burk got a job at a local sawmill after his release
from prison, but he was fired within a month after his hire.
The terminating of his services was, of course, not his fault
as will be shown shortly.

Having been fired at the sawmill, Burk had had
time to watch the activities at Payday Loan for the past two
months. He noted that, between ten a.m. and noon on the
days immediately before the first, and on the first, a female
employee would walk the two blocks to First National Bank
with a large deposit bag, and return with the bag which he
speculated was filled with cash. He attempted to follow her
into the bank to confirm what he suspected, but, on that occasion, the ever helpful bank receptionist intercepted him,
asking him if she could be of service. Burk ducked his head
and mumbled that he might be back later to open a new ac-
count, and fled the bank. Still, he remained confident that
his plan would work, and he would catch Payday Loan at
the zenith of its cash capacity.

"Why don't you get somebody else? I ain't much good
at stealing. I always get caught," Bugger continued anxiously
after getting no response from Burk.

Bugger, who received his nickname from an observant classmate when he saw Luther James enjoying his nose
pickings in Mrs. Haskins first grade reading class at Hern-
don Elementary School in Crow, presented an appearance
of anxiety most of the time when he was not pugnacious.
He had been a "Redbird" in Mrs. Haskins reading class, the
lowest of the bird groups, with "Bluebird" being the high-
est. Burk achieved Bluebird status, although he was several

years older than Bugger, and had not witnessed Bugger's failings in the reading class.

Bugger could still remember the painful swats on the palm of the hand with a wooden ruler wielded by Mrs. Haskins when he could not pronounce a word or mispronounced one. He had not fared much better with other local educators, and decided after spending ten years in the local schools, and achieving only eighth grade status, to drop out. The decision was not an easy one for the burly youngster as he learned that he could run fast with the football, and was well liked by most of his classmates, particularly those who received the same treatment as he did from the learned cadre at Crow Junior High School.

When Mrs. Shell made him stand and receive her mock applause for scoring *the worst score ever in the history of Crow Junior High School*, it was more than Bugger could take. Besides, she informed him that she would see that he was not eligible to play football any more. Bugger could see no further reason to continue his education. She had let the air out of his ball. He could not believe his coach, who tried to get him to remain in school could seriously believe that Mrs. Shell was simply trying to bring out the best in him by her ridicule.

Bugger and Burk became acquainted when Burk moved in with his sister, Letha Mae, and Letha Mae's two small children. Letha Mae worked as a waitress at Tooter's Cafe, a local cafe known as the best source of greasy food, and the latest town gossip. Like Bugger, she found the Crow education establishment was, at best, indifferent to her, but mostly contemptuous of her efforts.

When she developed breasts in the eighth grade, and

the principal became interested in tutoring her after school, Letha Mae determined that her schooling was at an end. She knew it was unlikely the citizenry would believe this education leader was pursuing a girl in his own daughter's class. Indeed, she was still trying to forget the pain and bewilderment she suffered when she attempted to tell the one teacher who had been kind to her.

The kind face had turned hostile, and told her "girls like you" always cause trouble. At that point in her young life, Letha Mae didn't know exactly what caused her to be a "girl like you," but she felt the hostility emanating from the only woman in whom she thought she could confide, and immediately ceased going to school, and no one challenged her decision.

Letha Mae's father worked in a local sawmill, and her mother did babysitting and housecleaning when she could get work. No one was overly concerned whether one of the many poor children in the area quit school; it was certainly not unexpected. She experienced a small glow of satisfaction, however, when two years after she quit her schooling, the principal and the *kind* teacher were caught unclad enjoying each other at the football stadium. Both moved on to other communities. Letha Mae wondered idly if the romance continued, but really didn't care. Other things occupied her time, part of which was her new romance with Joe Burk.

Occasionally, she wondered if she had now fulfilled the teacher's prophecy, and became a "girl like you." Whether it was true or not, she was dreading subjecting her sons to Crow's education system, even though she believed poor male children fared better in the system than poor female children.

Unlike her backward brother, she loved to read and had magnificent daydreams based on the romance novels she read when she wasn't working, taking care of her two small children, waiting on Bugger and Burk, or smoking marijuana. Letha Mae believed the weed used to make rope in days past enhanced her sexual abilities, and was always willing to experiment.

She, like her brother had wide shoulders, and both had dark curly hair, and very straight, white teeth. Men liked her, and she knew it. Little Todd and Tracy were proof enough. If she could only remember to make men put that rubber on, she wouldn't wind up pregnant. Still, she loved her two children, and with her waitressing wages, including tips, and food stamps, she was making it, she surmised, but wanted more than just making it. She wanted a taste of the life she saw on television sitcoms and in her magazines. If Joe doesn't go to work, and his crazy plan doesn't work, he's going to have to leave," Letha Mae promised herself for the hundredth time in two months.

After Burk was fired from the sawmill, Letha Mae had noticed he had not devoted himself to replacing the lost job. She sympathized with him when he was working at the sawmill. The owner regularly hired ex-convicts, particularly those on parole, who were required to keep a job. It was extremely difficult to keep workers on the green chain, a large conveyor belt that brought uncut logs into the mill. The man working the green chain had to grab one end of the log after it came past him, and using leverage, flip the log off, and then down the rollers which carried it to the next station. It was a continuous process, the logs were heavy, and if you let many slip by, you got fired. The work was hard on the hands, the shoulders, and the back, but more importantly for Burk, hard on the psyche. He felt, and knew, that he was nothing more than another machine for Jerry Cummins, the mill owner.

Cummins exacerbated this feeling by continuing to ask him, usually during the lunch break, when his co-workers were gathered together, whether he preferred the green chain to his comfortable prison cell with its color television, law library, weight room and other alleged social amenities. Burk thought several times about attempting to educate him and the others toward the harshness of prison life, but knew he was not going to change their perception of him or prison life. These men needed to feel that he was lower than they were, and although Burk was not privy to the psychological theories which made it so, he knew this fact, and was almost gladdened to provide this service for them.

Thinking of the worst day of his prison experience, Burk remembered being the sole witness to a murder in the prison weight room, and he knew the fear and trepidation he experienced that day would mark his personality forever. He had not told anyone about his observation of the event, and he, although now far removed from that particular prison, did not intend to tell anyone. He understood why Sonny Liston had not came out of his corner in Maine in the infamous fight between Liston and Cassius Clay, now known as Muhammad Ali. Liston, a former convict himself, said he was afraid only of a crazy man, and he viewed Cassius Clay to be a crazy man. Burk was convinced the murderer who stuck an ice pick in their fellow prisoner's head while he was lying down on a weight bench attempting to bench press three hundred pounds was also a crazy man. The weights dropped on the erstwhile power lifter's throat, and, after withdrawing the ice pick from the dead man's skull, the murderer looked at Burk and intoned in a monotone that one should never lift weights alone. Burk, noting he was the only other person in the room, made certain the dead weight lifter was, indeed, alone.

Certain he would never experience greater fear than when he looked into the killer's eyes, Burk knew, without another word being spoken between them, that he would never relate the circumstances of those few seconds to anyone else during his lifetime. The tragic *accident* in the weight room drew one paragraph in the *Daily Oklahoman* the following day. The newspaper cautioned that one should not lift weights alone.

Burk knew he did not want to return to any prison. There were too many people in the Oklahoma prisons who viewed life cheaply. Just one of those is too many if you are in the wrong place, he mused. His real fear, the one he would not even admit to himself, was becoming one of those crazies who viewed life cheaply. Burk remembered reading a German philosopher's view (someone whose name started with an N) that you had to be careful in destroying a monster so you did not become a monster. Burk did not want to return to prison.

Strangely enough, however, through his observations, the ex-convict reasoned without knowing why that he was going to have a better life than most of his sawmill workers, particularly those who had been at this mill for most of their life.

Cummins also knew Burk was contemptuous of him,

and the reason why. Cummins was a married man, and the father of two children. He was active in the Rotary Club, attended the Methodist Church on a regular basis—a pillar of the community. But every time he was able to address Letha Mae alone at Tooter's, or at other places, he attempted to get her to go out with him.

He asked Letha Mae to accompany him on an all expenses paid trip to Las Vegas, provided by a company from which he purchased machinery for his mill. He was prepared to tell his wife that it was a business trip, and he could not take her. God, when Letha Mae leaned over to serve him coffee, and he got a glimpse of her full breasts, he was ready to mortgage the mill to see the whole product. Letha Mae refused him, and continued to refuse him, and, he suspected she and Burk enjoyed laughs at his expense. He didn't care; because she had become an obsession with him, and he was used to getting his way. He certainly wasn't used to being upstaged by an ex-convict, and confirmed his suspicion on the date he fired Burk. A day Burk remembered well. Before Burk left that morning, Letha Mae told him Cummins hit on her the day before at the restaurant, and she told him to keep his business at home. Cummins approached the men, who were relaxing on their lunch break, and Burk was waiting on him.

"How's your love life, Cummins?" the impudent ex-convict inquired with a wide grin on his face.

Cummins knew he was, pursuant to the labor laws, required to give every employee a lunch break, but this was an added benefit of hiring parolees, Cummins calculated. He frequently had Burk doing menial tasks while the others enjoyed their lunch break. Who were they going to complain to? They needed their job to stay out of the prison, and were unlikely to complain, even to their co-workers.

When Burk made the inquiry about his love life, and there was raucous laughter among the men, it was evident to Cummins that Burk had told them about his failed overtures with Letha Mae. Cummins glared at Burk, and then at the men who seemed to be enjoying his discomfort and embarrassment. The laughter subsided. These men needed to keep their jobs, and ridiculing the owner was not in their best interests, notwithstanding they were delighted to hear about his failed efforts with Letha Mae. Her stock was at an all time high at the sawmill on that day.

"Burk, you can pick up your paycheck at the office. You're through here," Cummins said maliciously, giving Burk a cold stare.

The atmosphere was charged with tension as Burk arose with his fists clenched and stepped toward Cummins. With his eyes widened, Cummins involuntarily stepped back, ready to flee on a moment's notice. Burk noted Cummins' fear, and relaxed.

"You yellow piss ant," Burk said, punctuating the sentence with a wad of spit, which struck Cummins on the shoe. "You're not worth the trouble." Burk grinned again, pleased with his unexpected hit. Cummins reddened, but said nothing, glaring intently at Burk. Cummins knew he should answer Burk's challenge if he wanted to keep any respect from his laborers, but his fear of a physical beating by Burk overrode his need to keep their respect.

The men noted Burk's change of attitude and plan. Disappointment was the prevailing emotion. Even the men who didn't dislike their boss were not averse to seeing him pummeled by the personable ex-convict. Besides, who knows, the mill owner might have a change of heart and put up a fight. For men whose favorite television program was professional wrestling (most believed it was not fake), this looked like a real opportunity to see some live action. They knew Burk had won more than his share of battles at Sam's Drive-in, and other similar watering holes around the county. Without a word to Cummins or the other men, Burk strode past Cummins, and out the front gate. His sawmill career ended.

Thank God for overcrowded prisons, and the prison riot of two years before, Burk told Letha Mae after visiting his parole officer, and relating to him that he had been fired. The officer told him that he was giving him a break, and allowing him to remain out on parole while looking for work. He let it slip in the dialogue, however, that he didn't know where he would send Burk in any event, because the prisons in Oklahoma were overcrowded and already under a federal mandate to provide better conditions. There was speculation that the current conditions could result in another riot worse than the last one, which brought the state prisons under federal control. It also became apparent the officer knew of Cummins' practices, and had little regard for Cummins. Still, Burk knew he was going to have a hard time maintaining his conditions of parole, and began scheming to better his life and rid himself of parole restrictions and other confinements. He reasoned to himself, *I tried it their way, now I'll do it my way.*

CHAPTER

4

"WHAT DO YOU MEAN, you always get caught when you steal? You've never been to prison, or even county jail. At least, that's what you told me," Burk said, addressing Bugger's last communication.

"Momma caught me stealing my sister's lunch money once. Mrs. Dean caught me stealing a Coke in the fifth grade," Bugger said defensively.

Taking note of Burk's look of incredulity, Bugger continued, "I ain't stole much. I don't like what happens when you get caught." As an afterthought, he added, "You shouldn't either. Look what happened to you when you stole them cows. You don't want that to happen again, do you?"

"Hell no, and it won't happen again. Not if you do your part, and Letha Mae does hers," Burk stated flatly. He thought, "God, here I am planning my future with an idiot, and being lectured about not stealing. How much worse can it get? I've got to have him, dumb he might be."

Bugger knew how to hotwire cars, and although he claimed to have never stolen any, it was essential to Burk's plan that they have two cars to complete the robbery, with at least one that could not be traced to him or Bugger. He thought about the public perception that every ex-convict was an expert on stealing cars. Did they believe that Hot Wire 101 was taught on prison campuses across the state? He smiled wryly at the thought.

"I've told you before, I don't like people laughing at me," Bugger stated with some heat, misreading the smile. "What do you think is so funny?"

"Simmer down, pilgrim," Burk said, imitating John Wayne, as much as a not quite six foot, one hundred sixty-five pound, slightly bald man could accomplish. "I was just thinking about you teaching budding convicts how to hotwire cars in prison." He slapped Bugger on the shoulder and chuckled.

Bugger returned the smile uncertainly. He didn't like the part about prison, but it gratified him, made him feel good that Burk needed him.

The evening was a typical early evening for Little Dixie, as the southeastern part of Oklahoma was known to the rest of Oklahoma. The term was used with derision by other Okies who considered themselves more enlightened than the "rednecks" and "hillbillies" who chose to live in this part of the world. The humidity was thick enough to almost touch with your fingertips, and there was little or no breeze. Any physical effort of any consequence would result in sweaty bodies. The men favored Old Spice to ward off unpleasant odors, while women leaned toward Blue Waltz.

Burk remembered a sexual encounter he experienced

when he was nineteen that left him and his partner drenched in sweat. God, it was great. He wondered how his sex partner explained her sweaty bra and blouse to the grandmother she was visiting. Burk mused that he always had better luck with girls visiting from out of town than with the local belles. One visiting female attempted to insult him by telling she had just used him while she was in town. Because she was attractive, and good between the sheets, Burk hoped she told her similarly situated friends about his usefulness. "Go ugly early" was Burk's motto at the dances or bars on weekends; don't wait until the last dance or you might go home alone. He had broken his rule with Letha Mae.

When the State of Oklahoma decided to parole Burk, he took a bus from Taft, home of the Jess Dunn Correctional Center, to Crow. The song made popular by Tony Orlando and Dawn, or Orlando Tony and Dawn (Burk could never remember which) "Tie a Yellow Ribbon 'Round the Old Oak Tree" kept running through his head. The song told the story of a prisoner who, before being released, had told his wife that if she wanted him to come home, to tie a yellow ribbon around the old oak tree, and this would be the signal that she wanted him; if no yellow ribbon, he would "stay on the bus, forget about us" and keep going. The song's tale ended with a hundred yellow ribbons flowing from the tree, and the "whole damn bus" cheering. Burk knew there would be no yellow ribbons for him, and the old wino who kept ducking down to drink from his jacket, and the elderly woman reading her Bible who ignored him. He couldn't imagine either one cheering the fact that he left prison, and was going to make his home among them. Bus passenger traffic in

Little Dixie had slowed to a trickle, and would soon become non-existent.

Through the good services of his friend, Moses, he secured a room in a cheap hotel within walking distance of Cummins Mill.

Moses, fresh from his second divorce, suggested he and Burk go to the Broken Spoke the first weekend he was home and cast their lines to the females who were there to view what was available. The first female form which caught Burk's eye was Letha Mae's gyrating rear clad in a tight white mini-skirt as she participated in a twist oldie. Moses, noting his companion's interest, told him to go for it. When Burk told him he intended to find something very available (translation, ugly), and get himself bred, Moses just grinned and told him to not overlook the obvious. Burk, receptive to his friend's remark, invited Letha Mae to dance the next dance, which was another twist—the owner liked Chuck Berry.

Burk and Letha Mae performed with such enthusiasm that before the dance ended, there was a larger crowd watching them than dancing. It was obvious to the onlookers that Burk and Letha Mae were dancing a prelude to mating, and that the twosome were oblivious to the Broken Spoke crowd. For both, the dance ending was a disappointment. When a small smattering of applause broke out, both looked at each other, slightly embarrassed. Burk stayed beside her, and took her in his arms for the next dance, a slow "belly rubber." He invited Letha Mae outside for a drink of whiskey he and Moses brought and she accepted. Following the obligatory shot of whiskey, (neither being really interested in the liquor) Letha Mae and he did some heavy petting, and she agreed that he should take her home. Burk had, he told Moses later, struck gold, or at least, found a honey pot he did not intend to leave.

Letha Mae's memory of their first meeting was similar to Burk's. She spotted him shortly after the first twist oldie was history, and determined she would become acquainted with him during the *Sadie Hawkins* number if she had to resort to that tactic. The *Sadie Hawkins* number was the dance where the bandleader announced the next number would be the tune where the females asked the males to dance, a tradition carried over from the *Lil Abner* comic strip. Letha Mae liked everything she saw, and was glad Burk approached her as opposed to having to make the first move. It might make him easier to control later. She had already surveyed the available males before Burk showed up, and was almost ready to call the night a wasted night when he and Moses walked through the door. Burk reflected later when she told him this in a moment of honesty that he was glad he and Moses had hit some of their favorite drinking spots before going to the dance. She might have played hard to get earlier, and both would have missed out. Burk did not believe in chasing women, pretty or ugly, who pretended to not be interested. Heretofore, he never stayed long with any woman; after all, they were all the same in the dark, he stated many times. He found the deep unhappiness which came over him when he pondered leaving Letha Mae to be quite disconcerting. Never previously having a long time relationship with any woman, he convinced himself that he wanted no long time relationship.

Having to tell Letha Mae that he had no car on their first evening together and could not take her home, Burk was certain the heavy petting was all he was going to get.

"What do you mean you've got no car? Whose car is this?" Letha Mae asked flatly. Burk's mind raced. Should he tell her his car was in the shop? After all, he would probably never see her again, and a lie wouldn't hurt. He surprised himself by telling her the truth, even to the part where he just got out of prison. She surprised him and herself by telling him she had a car, and they could go home in it. All the while, Letha Mae was thinking, what is the matter with me? The last thing I need is to get mixed up with an ex-convict. She sensed however, that Burks' truth telling was very hard for him, and when she saw him looking straight ahead, and not at her, she knew he was preparing himself for her rebuff. She couldn't do it.

On the way home, she let Burk drive her car and sat closely beside him. Both were silent until she started giving him directions on how to reach her home. Burk was familiar with her part of town, he and his mother lived in some of the small houses nearby, and were evicted from one when one of Betty's binges lasted longer than usual. After stopping the car in the drive, he looked into her face and was surprised by the tender look she bestowed on him. It was disconcerting. Burk did not want tenderness; he wanted sex. Letha Mae gave him both.

CHAPTER

5

"LOOK, THE PLAN IS VERY SIMPLE," Burk said to Bugger. "Wednesday, we go to Texarkana and find a car you can hot wire. We can drive that car back, put it in the alley between Payday Loan and the shoe repair store and have it ready for the next day."

He examined Bugger carefully to determine the attitude and willingness of his would-be accomplice to participate in the grand adventure. Texarkana was the largest town close to Crow, and sat seventy-five miles away on the Texas-Arkansas line; approximately half of the city was in Texarkana, Texas, and the other half in Texarkana, Arkansas. Burk's only trip to Texarkana, Texas was to visit a whorehouse on the night of the prom when he was a junior in high school, but, he reasoned, it would be easier to steal a car in a town of 75,000 people than in Crow, or any neighboring town in Southeastern Oklahoma.

The heat was beginning to be less oppressive as

evening shadows lengthened, and Sam's drive-in lot began to fill up. Burk remembered studying a sixth grade geography book which listed the different climate zones in
the United States, and finding that the southeastern part
of Oklahoma lay in a different climate zone than the rest
of the state. The Kiamichi Mountains and the Ouachita
Mountains. which were directly north of the Crow area,
and the beautiful rivers and streams running through them
made this area a vacation paradise for those lucky enough
to learn of its existence. Burk had been told that Jimmy
Webb, the songwriter, wrote the song, "Wichita Lineman,"
made famous by Glenn Campbell as Ouachita Lineman, but
had to change it because no one would be able to pronounce
Ouachita. From the mountains, the land flattened until you
reached the Red River that separated Oklahoma from Texas.
Here, the farmers found the richest soil in Oklahoma in the
bottoms of Red River. Cotton had been the cash crop until
soybeans and other grains became more profitable. Marijuana was also a cash crop, which fared well in Little Dixie. In
later years, a Republican governor would infuriate the citizens in the southeastern tip of the state by stating that marijuana was the primary cash crop in McCurtain and Choctaw
Counties. Republicans were as scarce as hens teeth in Little
Dixie, and even when they told the truth, they were not well
received. George Wallace, the former Alabama segregation-
ist was very popular here in the elections in 1972 until his
campaign was ended by a gunman.

Burk continued, "Plan A is that if Josie Williams
is bringing the money back by herself, I will stop her. You
come in immediately behind her and we will escort her into
the alley, take the money, ask Miss Williams to get naked,

take her clothes, get in the car, and run like hell." He paused to check Bugger's reaction.

His idea of having Josie Williams divest herself of her clothes did not originate from any desire to see her un-clad, but, he reasoned, being naked in an alley in downtown Crow would disorient Josie long enough for them to escape without a hue and cry being made by her, and when she did venture out of the alley, enough attention would be paid to the shapely woman's body to buy them more time in driv-ing to meet Letha Mae at the designated hiding place and exchange cars.

"We ain't gonna hurt her, are we? You said nobody would get hurt. Ain't that right? YOU said nobody would get hurt," Bugger said, almost shouting the last sentence.

"Pipe down. Plan A will be the topic of conversation here tonight if you cain't be a little quieter," Burk said with some irritation.

Why did I pick this slug, he asked himself, knowing the answer before he completed the question. When he and Letha Mae devised their scheme, she insisted on Bugger be-ing his accomplice—even before Burk knew about his hot wire capabilities. She intended that her brother accompany them on the flight to Mexico, also, and let Burk know that any thought of leaving Bugger behind would be met with disfavor.

Letha Mae read that Americans with money could live like kings in Mexico—maids, servants, the whole works. Retirees were flocking to the country south of the border to live well, the ad stated in her romance magazine. American money was worth as much as seven times what it was in the United States. Joe Burk was going to be her ticket out of Crow, out of waitressing, out of waiting for the man who would treat her right, out of despairing that such a creature existed in Crow, or was likely to ever come there.

Don Wells, the man they were conspiring to rob, held much the same view of Crow residents as she did, she surmised. "They are either born here, or they come here," Wells had said. She took it to mean if they weren't crazy when they arrived, they soon would be. She liked Wells, and had engaged in many conversations with him at the cafe; he was one of the few who did not have roaming hands. Still, she felt no guilt or remorse at their plan to rob him. After all, she reasoned, Wells had more than he needed, and he was probably insured.

"Still, I don't want Josie to get hurt," Bugger said. "She was good to me at school." He remembered Josie coming up to him after an eighth grade football game in her cute cheerleader outfit and escorting him off the field. This happy event occurred the week before his humiliation in Mrs. Shell's class, and his subsequent exit from Crow Middle School.

Bugger went to the high school games and watched Josie perform until she got pregnant in her junior year, and had to quit cheerleading. He lost track of her until she began working for Payday Loans. For Bugger, the thought of seeing her sans clothes was one of the few appealing aspects of this scheme of his sister and Burk. What if she recognized him and wanted to go with him? His mind whirled at the possibility. But, how could she recognize him? Burk said they would be wearing masks and disguises. She might recognize him, anyway, he reasoned. After all, she had spoken to him at a football game several years ago. Maybe she felt the same way about him he felt about her, and was also afraid to approach him. The former eighth grade football star's head whirled with his unobtainable daydreams.

Burk continued, "Plan B will be to wait until Josie goes into Payday, and then both of us hit the place hard and fast. We'll lock the door behind us, point our guns at Wells—if he is there—and the rest, and make them strip. They can strip in them little stalls they use for making loans. We'll take the money Josie brought back, plus whatever they have at Payday." As an afterthought, he added, "And their clothes. They won't be too keen to chase us in their birthday suits."

He had gone over this with Bugger a hundred times, he felt, but reasoned, five hundred times might not be enough. Lord, he wished he had gotten somebody else—anybody would be better, he thought. The whole plan depended on no one recognizing him or Bugger, and the getaway being accomplished with speed and dispatch.

Plan B would bring in more loot, the brains of Crow's newest gang realized, but he opined it would also result in more risks. It was likely that borrowers would be there, and having to control at least three people, even with guns, presented some risks. Payday Loans was usually manned by Josie Williams and another employee—a black woman, Burk recalled. Wells never misses a trick; the black woman was there to bring in the black borrowers, a sizable population in Crow, Burk reasoned. Also, at this juncture in the month, it was likely that Wells himself would be there. A lot could go wrong. What if Wells decided to be a hero? Would he shoot him? Hell yes he'd shoot that son-of-a bitch. He'd kill them all if they fooled with him. Besides, Wells had a reputation of being a rich coward.

Burk heard that he had not served in World War II because he paid the recruiter to label him 4-F. He didn't know if it was true, but a lot of people said it was, and, in Crow, that was enough. Wells probably would not be a hero, but somebody else might. Hell, the black woman might. She looked like an Amazon, talked like a man, and Burk heard she collected from the toughest blacks in town.

Burk was having recurring nightmares ever since he and Letha Mae solidified their plan and picked an exact date. In the nightmare, he would attempt to shoot Wells, the gun would jam, and he would point it at Josie; the gun would explode and her head would pop off, blood spewing up from her headless frame. At this point, he would awaken, usually sitting straight up in bed.

Burk felt he knew himself well enough to know he was not naturally tough, but had taught himself to be tough to survive in his world. Even his reputation as a barroom battler was unearned, he felt. His mother's alcoholism had made him fear drinking, and as a result, he rarely was intoxicated, but many of his fights had been against drunks loaded with false courage, as hard drink was a norm well known in Little Dixie. He learned to disarm his opponents by smiling at them, and appearing to be backing off, and then landing the first punch, followed by a flurry of rights and lefts, and kicks, until he had won the battle.

The last battle had been hard on him because his opponent had scouted him, and was ready when he threw the first punch. It ended when Sam Stone fired a gun into the ground beside the two combatants and declared the fight was over.

Burk didn't know if Sam knew how glad he was to

see him, but both fighters complied, with each vowing to kill the other the next time they met. They had not met, and Burk did not know if the other battler was as happy as he was that they had not crossed paths. Still, he knew that to maintain his position in the circle of bars in the county, he would have to fight the challenger again, or quit frequenting the same watering holes.

The situation made the ex-convict think of the western movie where Gregory Peck, appearing as gunfighter Jimmy Ringo, returned to his hometown, wanting to see his son who didn't know Jimmy Ringo was his father. Ringo, however, was killed by a young punk who wanted to establish a reputation. Ringo, who hoped to quit being a gunfighter, lied to the marshall about the punk to force his killer to lead the life he had led. His son did not know Ringo was his father.

"Hell, I'm more like his kid than I am like Ringo," Burk thought. "I could quit fighting any time I wanted and I don't know who my father is. There's a lotta people going to these bars who never get in a fight. But those people don't have the reputation I do," he reflected. "I don't know if I can give that up."

Prestige was in short supply for the former star athlete after he left high school. *I've got to do something, be somebody even if it is just the best barroom fighter in Little Dixie,* he told himself. In rare moments of honesty with himself, he knew it was not enough. During his prison stay, and lately, he experienced problems fighting off ideas of suicide. He thought of Mark Twain's fictional character, Tom Sawyer, returning and visiting his own funeral where there were many weeping mourners. Few would mourn his passing, he thought bitterly many times before forcing his thoughts in different, if not always brighter directions.

After a short stint at Southeastern Oklahoma State University (about which more will be said later), Burk worked pipeline construction, highway construction, saw-mills, farms, and a multitude of short term jobs—until he and Steve Jones, a former teammate, determined they could acquire capital easily by stealing cattle. Jones, the son of a local small farmer, told Burk he knew cattle and how to steal and sell them. Their first foray into the life of crime ended in prison terms for both of them.

Burk and Jones let a new young lawyer, John Henry James, who had moved into town from Guthrie, Oklahoma, convince them that their athletic feats in the past would cause the jury to turn a blind eye to their theft, and even if they did convict, the sentence would be light. The young lawyer was extremely naive concerning the mindset of Southeast Oklahomans. John Henry was seeing Betty Burk, when he could convince his wife he had to work late, a *secret* known by most of the small town. The locals believed ball games were fun, but apprehended thieves were sure to get the worst treatment the jurors could administer. As a young lawyer, James got some valuable experience while Burk and Jones got prison sentences. Burk learned that past deeds are of little use when one's peers believe their cows might be the next cows stolen. Or your chickens, or your car, or your lawn mower, the District Attorney told the jury. Burk had to admit he covered all the bases. Shortly afterward, the young lawyer relocated back to Oklahoma City.

Burk's fervent hope was he would not have to shoot anybody, but if he had to shoot someone at the scene to accomplish his goal, he vowed to himself that he could. He would get the chance to test himself before the week ended.

Burk started Letha Mae's Maverick, the only car the family had. It was time for her to leave work, and she became unhappy when he showed up late, particularly if he had been drinking with her brother. She did not want Bugger to develop any bad habits.

Don Wells looked out from his second floor balcony at the early morning mist still hanging over the emerald green grass on his manicured lawn. He loved this time of the day. Except for the newspaper carriers, and those unfortunates who had to open the two restaurants in town which served breakfast, he was one of the few people not still in bed.

Wells usually awoke completely alert and ready to function. He could not understand his wife and daughter who wandered around in a daze for thirty minutes or more after they arose. His habit for the last several years had been to arise early, drive to his pastures out of town and check on his cows and horses. He would have preferred to live on the land where the animals were, but his wife insisted that Alyssa, their daughter, needed to live in Crow to get the full value of the social whirl. Wells knew he had few real friends in Crow, but didn't worry needlessly about this circumstance. He was born here, and liked the fact he was one of the richest men in town and, except for some traveling with his wife, Fay, did not intend to ever leave.

Wells often quoted Proverbs 6:10 to himself early in the morning, a Biblical verse which warned that sluggards who lay in bed instead of taking care of business would wind up in poverty and want. He knew it was unlikely that he was ever going to want for much, but it inspired him to take care of what he had. He liked the early morning drive to the pastures to check on the newborn calves, or to the horse barns to check on his prize quarter horses. "Barns" is a misnomer, Wells thought. The stalls had fans installed to keep the horses cool in the summer, and heaters to keep them warm in the winter. The Mexican who lived in the small room at the end of the barn told Wells that his horses lived better than most of the populace in the small village where he came from south of the border.

Although the jolt of the quarter horse's gait had become too much for his aging physique, Wells still loved to watch the awesome rippling of a really good cutting horse's haunches when the horse was going through a workout. He heard a football announcer compare a linebacker's maneuvering to a prime cutting horse and thought it the most wonderful compliment that could have been paid to the player, but the announcer 's partner—almost assuredly from New York—derided this comparison. The comment by the New Yorker, and the attitude of others in places he had visited, convinced Wells that his place in the world was in Little Dixie, and he didn't intend to leave it. He thought of the renowned artist who grew up in Crow, and named by *LIFE* magazine as one of the top ten artists in the world. *LIFE* described the artist's hometown of Crow, Oklahoma, as *quaint*. Wells felt quaint was an adjective reserved for New England towns, and was not descriptive of Crow whatsoever. Independent or rugged would have been much more accurate, Wells believed. Even *backwoodsy*, a term used by another writer would have been better. Quaint? Bull shit. When New Englanders write about the middle states, the reading public is stuck with their views, the businessman reflected.

Wells read in the *Crow Gazette* that a local lad who moved to Arizona had coached his football team to a state championship. *A lot of good people leave here every year,* he thought. *But a lot of good people still live here, too,* he asserted to himself.

He knew the state newspaper designated McCurtain County as one of the five most violent counties in the state, but neither he nor any of his long time companions were concerned about what a newspaper in Oklahoma City said about Little Dixie. Maybe the alleged violence would keep the come heres away, Wells reflected. He was well aware that there was a segment of the population who viewed fighting and violence as part of their heritage, and were proud of their Saturday night fights. It was a part of the Little Dixie mentality that he accepted, but did not care to join.

He was of the opinion that not every violent fatality in Crow or the surrounding communities was tragic. In his view, most homicides divested the community of two troublemakers by burying the victim and sending the perpetrator to prison. It rankled him that Sam Stone had not been tried and sent to prison in a shooting death at his bar.

His father owned one of the first banks in Crow, and Wells was still on the Board of Directors, although he was not active in the day-to-day administration of the bank. He found loaning money at 240% to the blacks and poor whites in Crow was much more lucrative. Also, by hiring two aggressive women who valued their jobs, he did not have to spend as much time at the loan company as he spent at the bank. Both employees were ambitious single mothers who, for whatever reason, did not want to leave Crow.

Josie Williams appeared to be a girl with everything

going her way in high school when she became pregnant. Being from one of the few Catholic families in Crow, Josie elected to not call on the services of the alcoholic doctor in Crow who performed abortions for those who needed it. Wells mused about this practitioner's livelihood since the nine old lunatics on the Supreme Court decided two years ago that abortion was to be available for everyone and legally to boot. *The country was going to hell in a handbasket,* Wells and the Church of Christ minister had agreed on several occasions. Wells had heard this alcoholic medical practitioner reel off the names of several young females who had utilized his services on a night at the local country club when the good doctor imbibed more than he should have.

Josie elected to not use his services, though it cost her dearly. There was much speculation about the father of the child, but she had kept her counsel concerning this secret. The former cheerleader graduated from high school, but the demands of motherhood combined with a poor family consigned her to the labor pool in Crow. She had been working for Payday Loans now for two years, and was Wells' best employee.

The other woman—Sylvia Murdock—was a large black girl who had been Crow's best basketball player during her school years until she became pregnant in her senior year. Wells knew Josie's religion kept her from the abortion practitioner, but he didn't know why Sylvia had not used the abortionist. He knew her brother regularly sold drugs, primarily to other blacks, and, it was rumored, also supplied some of the country club gentry with their needs and desires.

Wells rarely went to the country club although he

had been a member all his life. It always appeared to him that one-upmanship was the favorite game played there, and, for the most part, he knew he could win ninety-nine percent of those matches, but it didn't seem worthwhile to play. The evening when the abortionist chose to reveal some of his secrets was the last time he was there, which was to please his wife who wanted to go with their daughter to announce the daughter's intention to enter medical school after graduating from the University of Oklahoma.

Wells knew that the father of Sylvia Murdock's child attempted to marry her, but she declined his offer. She and the father appeared to be on good terms. Why she would not marry him was her own business. Collections from the black community had never been better, and Wells was determined to keep the former basketball player on his payroll. He found some guy representing himself to be from Southeastern Oklahoma State University talking to Sylvia the week before—something about Title IX. Wells didn't know what Title IX was, but he knew Sylvia still played basketball in some kind of church league. He told the university recruiter that if he wasn't there to borrow money, he needed to leave, knowing the recruiter would almost certainly see the large woman at home. God, if these crazy women libbers would just leave things alone, Wells thought, everything would be so much more settled and comfortable. His church, the Church of Christ, still believed in women keeping in their place, thank God.

He felt estranged from his own daughter almost from the first day she went to Norman to be a student at the University of Oklahoma, known in Little Dixie as the tea-sippers' school, and a hotbed of liberalism. If the OU

Sooner football team and their new coach, Barry Switzer, could be separated from the rest of those longhairs who infested the university, Wells and most of Little Dixie would be very happy.

Now, his daughter was unmarried and practicing medicine in Oklahoma City. He knew most people thought he should be proud of her, but he would have preferred her to marry some local boy who could help him with his farms and other businesses. The plans of mice and men really do go awry, Wells thought.

CHAPTER

6

ON THE OTHER SIDE OF TOWN, Burk had also arisen. Like Wells, he rarely slept late. Bed was a place to sleep and make love, not spend the day. No emerald green lawn met Burk's eye, however, as he stood on the rickety front porch and peered at the white gravel street in front of the small two-bedroom wooden house with peeling green paint. What grass there was on the property was a hardy variety that survived despite the weeds, and was mowed only when the city threatened the inhabitants. He drank deeply from the coffee cup he held in his hand, and pulled on the Pall Mall cigarette. Letha Mae could not understand his reluctance to join her when she mellowed out on marijuana. Burk the battler did not want her to know that, having seen his mother lose all her bouts with liquor, he wanted to insure he did not become addicted to anything, even a little harmless *happy tobaccy*. Even his cigarette smoking was limited. The son of the alcoholic mother was determined to not be attached to anyone or anything.

A clanging noise inside the house assured him Letha Mae was preparing breakfast. Scarcely thirty feet away to the west of him, he heard another woman making pot and pan noises. Luke Brown's wife was up getting his breakfast ready. Burk worked with Brown at Cummins Sawmill, and liked him. The small house to the east remained dark. A black family lived there, and insofar as Burk knew, none of the group who lived there worked. This was a poor neighborhood, but Burk could remember when no blacks would have dared to live there. He had almost no thoughts whatsoever about integration one way or the other. He played football, basketball and baseball with blacks in the Army during the time he was a warrior for Uncle Sam, and likewise, played the same sports with the black population at the various prisons in Oklahoma for the past five years.

All D.O.C., he told Bugger when he first met him, and Bugger was boasting of his eighth grade football prowess. When Bugger inquired what it meant, he told him it meant he was an All Department of Corrections player, grinning to let Bugger know it was a joke. Bugger did not comprehend it as a joke, and he later heard Bugger bragging to someone at Tooter's about his sister's boyfriend being All D.O.C. A good laugh was had by all listeners in the small cafe. Ah, well, fuck them. I'm not going to be here long, anyway, Burk thought. He thought about the bodybuilder contest when he was in prison in western Oklahoma, an event he won. Quite an achievement, he thought wryly.

The theft of the extra car did not go as Burk planned. He and Bugger drove around Texarkana for hours before Bugger announced that a 1957 Ford was to be the car of choice. When Burk inquired why he wanted to steal such an old car, Bugger told him it was the only model he knew how to hot wire. Burk, ignorant of such matters, threw up his hands and told him to go for it. Bugger, true to his word, after finally locating a 1957 Ford, knew how to get the old car started without the benefit of a key, and now the two-toned brown Fairlane was parked behind the house.

"Come in, honey, breakfast is ready,"Letha Mae said, appearing at the front door. She was holding the screen door open with one hand, and holding back her hair with the other hand. The screen was torn, and brushed against her bare leg. She was wearing a short negligee that covered little, and her large white breasts appeared ready to pop from the silky covering at any minute. Burk knew she was a sexual fantasy for ninety percent of the regulars at Tooter's Cafe. A little something for the hand late at night when even the girls known as dogs didn't want to play, he thought. His loins reacted to the sight before him. He went to her and pulled her close to him.

"I said breakfast is ready, and that's all that's ready," Letha Mae said, but she was smiling. She knew Burk's reputation as an ex-convict and a loser, but she also knew other things, which made him outstanding in her eyes. She complained delightedly to one of the other waitresses that Joe could fuck forever. He never hit her, and his patience with Todd and Tracy was something she had not counted on when she allowed him to take her home from the dance at the Broken Spoke Club. A man who didn't beat women, and did not bully small children was a rare find in Letha Mae's circle of acquaintances. She also knew, however, they could not have much of a future if they stayed in Crow.

God, if this deal could come off today, and they really could make it to Mexico, even for a little while. She was really sick of this little town, the grabby customers, the cheap hustlers, and the bleak future she saw for herself if she stayed here. *Even if we only get away with it for a month, it will be worth it,* Letha Mae said to herself.

Besides, in her mind, she had been building a defense. She had feelings for Joe Burk, probably more than she ever let herself feel for anyone else, but she viewed herself as a survivor; she was certainly willing to testify it was all Burk's doing if they were caught. He only invited her, her brother, and her kids to accompany him to Mexico, is what she was planning to say if and when they got caught.

She already packed a suitcase and put it in the trunk of the car, although Burk told her to pack nothing. His plan was if law enforcement agencies set up roadblocks, he didn't want anything inside the car or the trunk to arouse the suspicions of the police. He told her it would appear the family was simply out for a drive, or a short trip. He told her that she and the children would be the icing on the cake for the getaway. The cops would be looking for two men, not five people, and certainly not a woman with two small children accompanied by her common-law husband and retarded brother.

She balked at the common law husband bit, and also at the part about not taking any clothes, especially for the two youngsters, but he insisted, and her greed overcame what she viewed to be common sense, that is, even a family out for a short trip would pack a suitcase. She agreed, and even sewed together some boxer shorts with elastic to fit around the boys' legs, the idea being that the loot would be stuffed in each boy's shorts. Burk assured her cops would not search the underwear of small boys. Still, Letha Mae was not going to leave home without packing something for herself and the boys.

Early that morning, in the total darkness engulfing the car at three a.m., she stowed her suitcase in the trunk of the car. Having seen the movie, *The Getaway*, she fantasized herself in the Ali McGraw part as the slender, sexy gun-toting partner of Steve McQueen who helped him in all of his harrowing escapes. Joe does look something like Steve McQueen, thought Letha Mae, but I am afraid I resemble Sally Struthers, the hostage victim, more than I do Ali McCraw, she reflected, laughing at herself. God, I hope I don't have to go through any harrowing escapes, anyway; just clear sailing to Mexico, and the good life.

She reflected for a moment about the irony of bringing God into her hopes for a successful crime. Her experience with religion left the bosomy waitress skeptical about its value. She was determined to become religious after quitting school, and started working at Tooter's where she quickly found the men who frequented the place were even more sexually aggressive than the junior high school principal had been.

She reasoned the godly men at the First Church of the Faithful had to be different than the grabby customers she saw every day, and she thought the regulars at the cafe might not pursue her so heatedly if they thought she had visions of nunnery, or the holiness church version of the same.

The stars of this charismatic group at the First Church of the Faithful would get high spiritually every Sunday, and venture to the front of the sanctuary to talk in what was known as unknown tongues. Some convinced themselves that their unknown tongue was a direct link to God, and some wanted to be a part of this elite group with the inside track to God. Letha Mae couldn't understand their wailing, but it looked like fun, and she joined them one Sunday morning. She was spouting gibberish with the best of them after joining the huddle, and soon, she was one of the Sunday morning regulars. She began to realize, however, when it came time for laying on of hands and prayer, these godly men were sneaking the same feels the customers at the cafe were attempting. Still, it was exciting, and she might have continued indefinitely if a traveling redheaded evangelist had not been attracted to her. When he asked her to stay for extra prayer after the Sunday night service, she looked at his piercing eyes and the bulge in front of his pants, and consented. The man who had given a stirring sermon scant moments before was ramming the fear of God into Letha Mae on the carpet in front of the altar in rapid bursts when his spouse and the wife of the local pastor entered the sanctuary, ostensibly to see if the godly evangelist had helped the poor waitress pray about her wickedness. Letha Mae was dechurched the following Sunday, and never been back. She saw the redheaded evangelist occasionally on Sunday mornings on local television in Texarkana, still giving stirring sermons. Occasionally, the camera would flip to the devoted, demure wife engrossed in her husband's sermons, sitting on the front row.

Letha Mae rationalized her disloyalty to Burk by telling herself that she had to think of her two children, and, besides, he told her that she shouldn't count on him, that he was likely to be gone any morning when she woke up. Why shouldn't she look out for herself? It was certain no one else was going to, she reasoned matter of factly.

"No appetizer before breakfast? It wouldn't take long, a real quickie," Burk leered.

"No, honey. I hear Bugger and the kids stirring. Wait until tonight and we can do it in a foreign country," she, said, pulling Burk against her.

He looked at her wide forehead, down to her breasts, and sighed, "All right. I can wait. I'm going to need all my strength today. Anyway, I don't want to pour half of it into you."

"If a *quickie* is going to take half your strength, maybe I better find me a better man," she sassed at him as she popped him playfully with her fist, and walked back toward the kitchen/dining room. Todd, Letha Mae's four-year-old son was seated at the table drinking a Coca-Cola from a bottle. His blonde hair was tousled, and sleep was still evident in his face, but he was alert, and watching his mother and Burk. His mother was usually gone during this time of day, and he was usually still asleep in the bedroom he shared with his three-year-old brother, Tracy. Tracy was also at the table with his head on his forearms on the table, unaware of what was happening in the small room which served as the kitchen/dining room.

Breakfast was a Sunday event for these two small boys. Their mother was gone to her waitressing job at Tooter's by five a.m. every day of the week except Sunday, and their morning meal was usually cereal and soda pop prepared by Bugger at a much later hour of the day. Tracy was much darker than his brother, Todd, and was obviously the product of a coupling with one of the Choctaw Indians in the area. Although prejudice against the blacks in Crow was still evident in most of the population, Burk's view was the Choctaw Indians suffered little, if any prejudice.

He had been to Wyoming to work on a construction job, and attempted to enter a local restaurant with Moses Wills, a Choctaw Indian boy who worked with him (the same fellow who became the target of Sam Stone years later). The Wyoming restaurant owner informed Moses that he could not eat there, and Burk's argument that Moses was an Oklahoma Indian carried no weight in Wyoming. The restaurant owner told them he didn't care if he was an Oklahoma Indian, an Arkansas Indian, a Texas Indian, or a fucking New York Indian; he wasn't going to be served in his restaurant. Burk didn't know if all those states even had Indians, but when he noticed the restaurant owner slide his hand into an open drawer, he and Moses decided the local Dairy Freeze was an okay place to eat.

He and Moses had been to every eatery in Crow, and all of the bars in the county, and no one ever brought up the question of race. Sam Stone's shooting at Moses had nothing to do with race; it was just that Moses tended to get loud and belligerent when he was drunk.

Burk played baseball for an independent team which was all Indian, although he didn't realize it until he went to play in a tournament in Talihina and overheard his coach talking to another coach when he ran to field a ball behind first base. The Talihina coach asked Burk's coach where he recruited the *white kid*. Burk looked around, and realized he was the only *white kid* on the field. He thought about it for a millisecond, and went back to playing ball. As far as he was concerned, he was on the best independent team in

Crow, and whether they were Choctaw Indians, or Eskimos didn't matter to him.

"Git up, Bugger. This is our big day," Burk said with forced enthusiasm. He was having second thoughts about the planned robbery. Dark thoughts permeated his soul; robbery was not pumping adrenalin into his psyche.

Bugger was asleep on the divan that made out into a bed in the living room of the small house. On most nights, Bugger preferred to fall asleep watching television and rarely opened the divan. He was fully clothed, having fallen asleep in his clothes the night before.

Looking at the disheveled, sleepy, retarded twenty-year-old man-child, Burk felt even more like he was caught in the current of a river of circumstances that was sweeping him toward disaster. He couldn't think of any way to back out now without having to leave Letha Mae. What began as an offhand remark to her about hitting the loan company when they had the most money available had been adopted as her dream, and he was the dream fulfiller.

"Do I have to really carry a loaded gun," Bugger inquired anxiously of Burk, still sitting on the sofa/bed.

"Hell, yes, you have to carry a loaded gun. If we have to go into the loan company, I intend to shoot into the ceiling as soon as we enter the door to let them know we mean business. You do the same right behind me, and it'll scare the shit out of all the sane people in there. Yes, you have to carry a loaded gun, and you have to shoot it." Burk almost yelled, advancing toward Bugger as he spoke.

"Joe, you don't have to bully him. He'll do it. Won't you, Luther?" Letha Mae pleaded with her younger brother. She refused to call him by his nickname all of their life, although it is doubtful anyone else in town knew his real name.

Bugger looked sullenly at his sister. In his mind, he owed her for his very existence. When his mother threw him out of her house, his sister took him in, and now even paid him for babysitting her children. His babysitting skills included turning on the television, finding cartoons he liked, and watching them with the two boys.

Letha Mae failed to tell him that he was being paid with his own money. She knew Bugger was not ever going to be able to get a regular job. With her help, he applied for Supplemental Security Disability, a government program for people who could not get or hold a job anywhere in the United States. Bugger was approved to receive the benefits, but needed a payee to take care of it for him. She was named as his payee, and now doled money out to him as she thought prudent—and also depending upon her needs, the children's needs, and, on Saturday nights, her desire for marijuana. I wonder if the Government will send his check to Mexico, Letha Mae pondered. Burk and others called the government largesse Bugger's "crazy check," but Letha Mae warned him and others not to discuss the money with her brother. She didn't consider her actions deceitful, and viewed herself to be her brother's mother as much as she was Todd's and Tracy's mother.

"All right. I'll tote the gun, but I don't want Josie to get hurt," Bugger said, looking with emphasis at Burk when he mentioned Josie.

"Good God! That gal don't even know you're still alive. Besides, she and ole' Banks will probably have worn themselves out in the bank elevator before she returns with the money. She won't have any energy to do anything," Burk said, noting the look of distress and dismay on Bugger's face. "Hell, she may not have to work too hard to undress. Particularly if she left any of her clothes in the elevator."

Burk knew one of the other female tellers had inadvertently walked into Dennis Banks' office at the bank and found Josie Williams and Banks locked in an amorous embrace. Clothes were straightened in a hurry, the observant teller quickly reclosed the door, and Josie exited the office without looking at the door opening teller. It didn't take long for the story to make the rounds at the bank, then to Tooter's, and to the other watering holes in Crow. The other tellers then began to remember the unexplained elevator trips to the second floor taken by the pair, particularly the day the elevator got stuck for more than an hour with only the loan company employee, and the bank's youngest vice-president inside. Dennis Banks was hired away from a bank in Mt. Pleasant, Texas, and was viewed by the town's gentry as a young man with a future.

"You shut up! You don't know anything, and Josie does like me. Just shut up!" Bugger shouted the last words. Burk, keyed up about the plans for the day's big event, and apprehensive about what was going on in his life, felt a trigger go off inside.

He decided to teach the man child a lesson, and advanced toward Bugger only to be met head on by Letha Mae.

"Joe, don't do it. You'll ruin everything," Letha Mae said, holding onto Burk's upper arms and pushing back. "You know he's got this thing about that girl, and he can't stand you talking trash about her."

She felt Burk's biceps moving back and forth, and

then relaxing. "Thank God," she muttered to herself. "All we need is for these two to get into a fist fight, and beat themselves up before getting into the car to rob Payday Loan together. And they are going to rob Payday," she continued thinking determinedly, "no matter what I have to do to get it accomplished."

Noting Bugger had not moved, but, at least, he had not advanced toward Burk. Letha Mae knew of Burk's reputation as a barroom battler, but thought, Joe could have met his match here. Bugger did not seek fights, but she knew he was strong, and knew no fear. She, feeling Burk's arms loosening, turned her head toward Bugger, keeping her hands on Burk.

"Luther, don't be so sensitive about that Josie Williams. There will be plenty of Mexican senoritas willing to make your acquaintance when we show up with money," she said, giving him her most winning, white-toothed smile. She knew she had won him over when he smiled back.

"Okay, okay, but I still like Josie," Bugger said.

"So does Dennis Banks," Burk said, not being able to resist getting in a parting shot.

An irritated look crossed Letha Mae's face. Burk spotted it and put his arms on top of her arms, which she still had outstretched keeping him back.

"Okay Letha Mae, it's no skin off me if your brother wants to *looove* Josie, and I sure as hell don't care who Josie *loooves*. Bugger, I'm sorry if I insulted your girlfriend," Burk said, detaching himself from Letha Mae, and stepping toward Bugger with his hand outstretched. Bugger took the hand offered to him

"She ain't my girlfriend. I just like her."

Burk looked to Letha Mae for guidance. She shrugged, and smiled.

"Whatever," said Burk. "Let's eat."

The ominous feeling Burk had at breakfast continued when he and Bugger went into the backyard to start the 1957 Ford. The car wouldn't start, notwithstanding Bugger's earnest work under the dash.

"What's the matter? Did you forget how to start the thing?" Burk inquired, thinking dejectedly that he should never have entered into this deal with Bugger and his sister.

"Sounds like your battery is dead and gone," Burk heard a voice from a distance say. "You want a jump?"

Burk looked at the speaker, and saw it was the black man from next door. "Oh, God, this really tears it," he thought. "Do I tell him, yeah, we just stole this thing, and now we can't get it going, and we really need it to rob the local loan company?"

Bugger saved him the trouble of responding. "Hello, Elmo. Yeah, if you got some cables, we could sure use a jump."

Burk looked at his crime partner, who was grinning. Apparently Bugger and Elmo were good friends. "What the hell," Burk allowed to himself. "We've got to get this thing started, and moved even if we don't rob the loan company. It wouldn't do to have a stolen car in one's backyard, probably against a Crow city ordinance," he thought. He held out his hand and approached the black man, who was dressed in a sleeveless undershirt, jeans, and bare feet. Fuzz of a dingy white color hung in Elmo's mustache, which drooped to his chin.

"I'm Joe Burk. Yeah, we sure could use a jump. You

live next door here," Burk said, forcing a smile. In prison, segregation was still the rule, and Burk felt prison had the better plan when dealing with the races.

"Naw, I was listening to the police scanner, all about these white boys stealing a car, and thought them boys are probably going to need a black brother to help them get it started," Elmo said, looking directly into Burk's eyes, and squeezing the hand Burk offered.

A black wise ass, Burk flashed, this is going to be perfect day. He withdrew his hand.

"Well, Elmo, I guess you're going to have to decide whether to be a good citizen, and turn in these white boys. I think they're offering a Zero candy bar as a reward—or you can be a really good neighbor, jump this car, and help us to get the hell out of here." Burk said, returning the direct stare of the jumper cable owner.

"I heard it was a Hershey bar. If it was a Zero, your ass would be in a slingshot going to Big Mac. I love them Zero bars," Elmo said, still not smiling. Big Mac was a reference to the prison at McAlester, the oldest institution of incarceration in Oklahoma. Only the hardcore criminals were sent to McAlester, but Death Row was located there, and mothers, teachers and other persons intending to frighten young boys into behaving still invoked Big Mac as a way to get the attention of recalcitrant youngsters. Burk had never been to Big Mac.

"What about them jumper cables? I'll get Letha Mae's Maverick if you'll get those cables. I'm sure glad the cops favor Hersheys as rewards," Burk said, realizing Elmo had no intention of calling law enforcement. *Hell, he's probably on parole, too,* Burk reflected. *I'll soon know.*

"Elmo? Is that your name?" Burk queried. "I heard Bugger call you that. Didn't we do time together—either Granite or Hodgens? You sure look familiar."

"Boy, I ain't ever done time, and I don't intend to do time. I just don't need no stolen cars next door to me. These honky cops might try to link us up. I used to watch you play ball. You sure fucked yourself up, and now you are going to fuck up this boy, and his sister. But it ain't none of my business. I'll get them cables, and be glad to be rid of you in this neighborhood. Cause you won't be coming back," Elmo said, turning to go toward his car.

Burk's face turned red. Who did this nigger think he was, talking to him like that? He looked at Bugger, who remained silent through the conversation. Bugger was still trying to determine why his sister's boyfriend and Elmo were discussing candy bars.

"Fuck you! I'll come back when and if I want to. You sure as hell won't have anything to do with it." Burk said, belligerently.

Elmo continued his trek toward his car, ignoring Burk. He opened the trunk of his car, retrieved the cables, and started back toward the two white men and the stolen car. Burk, seeing him returning with the cables, glared at Elmo, but went to the front yard to get Letha Mae's car.

"What else is going to go wrong?" he asked himself. "I should just back out of this whole mess and go my way. God, I hate to leave Letha Mae, though. I don't know where I'm going to find anything like her. Hell, the whole town thinks she's a whore, and I'm pining about losing her."

Aside from the great sex he was enjoying with her, however, he found Letha Mae enjoyed his sense of humor and read almost as much as he had. Burk stated many times that he didn't know what "love" was, but he really enjoyed Letha Mae. *She really wants this thing to come off, and get to Mexico. I'll make it happen,* he said to himself, setting his jaw.

After starting the Maverick, Burk guided it down the grassy path between their house and Elmo's, noting that Elmo was walking beside him with the jumper cables. *"Police scanner, my ass,"* he thought. *There wouldn't be anything on a police scanner in Crow about two white males stealing a 1957 Ford in Texarkana. How could this nigger know the car was stolen?*

He looked ahead at Bugger standing by the raised hood on the 1957 Ford with a look of perpetual anxiety on his face. Then, like a light bulb in a cartoon, Burk realized why Elmo knew the car was stolen. Bugger told him. Hell, that also made the remark about him not coming back make sense. Bugger must have told him about the plans to rob the loan company too. *Good God, I wonder if the Crow Gazette also knows, and plans to have a photographer there,* Burk questioned in disgust. Glancing into Elmo's back yard, he spotted a 1957 Ford much like the one he and Bugger stole in Texarkana; he now knew why Bugger 's expertise on hot wiring was limited to 1957 Fords.

He got out of the car, approached Elmo and said, "It's occurred to me that our mutual friend here has been confiding in you about our plans for today. I don't much care what he's told you. I do care what you intend to do about it," Burk said, probing with his eyes into the black man 's soul.

"I don't know anything, I don't want to know anything, and I hope Bugger, his sister, and her kids get good suntans wherever they're going on vacation. If they shoot your ass, don't expect me to sing at your funeral," Elmo said, spitting on the ground near Burk's left foot to punctuate his last remark.

"You sure don't seem to care much for me. What did I ever do to you?" Burk said, genuinely puzzled by the neighbor's animosity toward him.

"Man, you were a poor boy who had a chance to make good, a real chance. You blew it, and I think you hurt every boy's chances in this poor town to make it out of here," Elmo said, emotion making his face drawn and intense.

Burk's mind raced, trying to think *of a real chance* he ever had to leave Crow and make good. "You talking about the scholarship offer I got to play football at Southeastern?" Burk queried, still trying to determine why this man didn't like him.

"Yes, I'm talking about your yellow ass not even making it through two-a-days before you drug back to Crow. When they talked to my boy, the first thing they said was that Crow boys didn't last long, and they thought they'd give their scholarship to somebody else," Elmo said. "You not only fucked it up for yourself; you fixed it where it will be a long time before any Crow boy gets another chance."

Elmo's words carried Burk back to an earlier period of his life. He flashed back to the hot August days he spent on the football field at Southeastern Oklahoma State University in Durant. He arrived there out of shape; indeed, with a hangover from having celebrated his going away the night before at Sam's Drive-In.

He discovered the scholarship offer included jobs, such as cleaning the gymnasium, and he would have to borrow money to make up the difference between what the scholarship paid, and what it did not pay. He knew no one who would loan him money. Moreover, football on this level was a job, and not fun as it had been in high school. Curfew was strictly enforced, and drinking at the local bars could cause you to be ousted from the team.

Burk left the second week when L.P. Andrews showed up after the evening practice with two good time girls headed for Athens, Georgia, to work on a pipeline. Burk slipped out of the athletic dormitory, got drunk with L.P., Janie and Susie, and woke up in Mississippi on the way to Georgia. He called the coach from a diner in Mississippi, but after being told he faced disciplinary measures, hung up the telephone and continued to Georgia. Too bad because he felt he was going to make the team, although not in the way he wanted to. His high school success had not prepared him for the competition at the college level.

He remembered the second day in pads when a punt was kicked to him and he started to the right, saw the opposition driving hard toward him, then cut back left diagonally across the field, zipping past the defenders as each tried to put on the brakes and change direction. It was a move he made many times in Crow, usually with success. He was flying without wings when he hit the left sideline and knew he would score as he had done many times for Crow High School. No problem. Then, this blur came from nowhere and caught him at the ten yard line. Southeastern's first black recruit caught him from behind. Burk couldn't believe it; he had never been caught from behind. The coach talked to him after practice about a future in the defensive backfield. Burk remembered his loss of confidence, his uncertainty and confusion. He was certain football at Southeastern would be little different than Crow High School, but having to change his image of himself, and become a defensive back was discouraging. Thus, when L.P. showed up, he didn't take long to chuck the whole college football thing and go where the wild goose goes. Occasionally, he reflected that his whole life would have been better had he chosen to stay and tackle runners instead of being a runner. He thought, *Water under the bridge now. No use worrying about it.*

He was unaware that anyone from Crow knew, or cared why he left. His story to the locals who inquired about why he left was he had torn cartilage in his knee, and could no longer play.

"Hey, I don't even know your boy, but don't blame me for him not being good enough to play at mighty Southeastern. They went 0-10 last year. It's probably good for your boy he wasn't there. And don't call me yellow. I may show you just how red I can make you," Burk said, working himself up to take on this unfriendly neighbor who made him relive part of his past; a part he did not want to remember.

Elmo looked to be in his late forties or early fifties, but was not fat nor skinny. He was taller than Burk, and twenty pounds heavier. Burk's bluster did not seem to faze Elmo.

"Boy, I jist ain't got time to be messin' with you. Do you want to start that car, or are you goin' to back out on that deal, too?" Elmo said, speaking in a tone that parents use for unruly two-year olds. Burk's face reddened, and he clenched his fists. The squeaking sound of the back screen door opening distracted the would-be combatants.

"Joe, please just start the car. Don't be getting in

fights this morning. We ain't got time," Letha Mae said from the back door of the small house. She had been watching the activities from the time Burk started her Maverick. Turning to Elmo, she smiled. Burk noticed she was wearing a short black mini-skirt, a tight white top, dark hose, earrings, bright lipstick, and bracelets. *She does clean up well,* he thought.

"Elmo, how you doin'? We appreciate you helping us start this car we just got, don't we, Joe and Luther?" Letha Mae trilled, using every bit of her femininity.

The three men, entranced by her well-formed legs jutting out of the mini-skirt, the breasts accented by her sideways stance in the door, or her smile, or all combinations, looked at her and at each other. No one commented that everybody in the group knew the 1957 Ford was stolen; it just didn't seem appropriate. If this well formed woman wanted it to be a car that her men just obtained, Elmo was not going to question this bit of illogic.

"Yes, ma'am. I've got my cables, and we's going to start this car. You jist go ahead, and get those boys ready. This car's gonna be rolling in a minute. Right, boys?" Elmo grinned at Burk and Bugger as he spoke.

Golly, ol' Elmo's in love with her. What do you know, thought Burk. His momentary anger at Elmo subsided, and he felt almost a kinship with him.

Bugger's head swam. A minute ago, he thought his sister's lover and his neighbor were going to fight. Now, they seemed to be long lost friends, both smiling, and simpering at his sister.

Letha Mae, certain the situation was defused, backed through the door and closed it. *How the hell does he know*

I'm getting my children ready, she questioned herself in the kitchen mirror. *Has my simpleton brother told him everything?* She debated about whether to tell Joe to just call it off. Looking at herself in the mirror, she made up her mind quickly. *Hell no, we won't call it off. We can pull this off and have a great time in Mexico, and we're going to do it. But what about Elmo?*

Letha Mae and Bugger had become well acquainted with Elmo Breed before the arrival of Burk, and she knew his history. He told her some of it, and her inquiries revealed even more. Elmo's father fatally shot a white farm couple near the Red River during the depression. Elmo told her the white sharecroppers cheated his father, causing him to be evicted from the farm that the white couple occupied at the time of the killings. Elmo's last memory of seeing his father outside of jail walls was when he ran into the small house of his family, told his wife he had killed the Joneses, and he was heading for Texas. His father was captured in Texas after one of the largest manhunts in Southeastern Oklahoma and Northeastern Texas. The sheriff spirited the killer away in the darkness of night to avoid an army of citizens who were determined to hang him without benefit of trial. The sheriff was soundly defeated in his re-election bid the following summer. Elmo's father was electrocuted by the State of Oklahoma in October, 1935; he killed the white sharecroppers in February, 1935. Lengthy appeals were not in vogue at the time.

Elmo remembered the newspaper reporting that his father, in the week before the execution, stated he didn't feel the state should take his life; that every man should be given the chance to live his seventy and seven years as the

Bible proclaimed. Elmo didn't know whether his father was begging to be spared, or was being defiant. He preferred to think of him as defiant.

Elmo had, himself, killed a man. After he returned to Crow, and his wife left him, he had been drinking heavily at a local bar frequented only by blacks when he and a "townie" got into an argument. Elmo remembered being amazingly calm as he walked away from the argument in the bar, and went outside to his pickup. The would-be combatant followed him to the pickup. When Elmo pulled the rifle off the rack in the back window of the pickup, all of the loiterers who followed the pair outside fled except James Harrell, a life long friend of Elmo's. He remained to try and dissuade Elmo from using the gun. Elmo looked directly into his tormentor's eyes, and told him that he was going to count to ten before he began shooting; giving him a chance to run as far and fast as he could. The intended victim—now convinced and frightened—wasted the first two counts trying to persuade Elmo not to shoot, but, quickly seeing the futility of argument, fled on the count of three. Elmo fired into the darkness at the count of ten. The victim's body was found sixty yards away from where he began his last run. Harrell told the sheriff's investigator that he struggled with Elmo, and the gun discharged accidentally. *All* others said they had ran back inside, and saw nothing. There was speculation about whether Elmo had that many friends, or if their knowledge of the Breed propensity for fatal violence caused them to color their recollection of the night 's events. The story was accepted; Elmo's calculation was the white sheriff didn't really care whether blacks killed each other every Saturday night as long as they didn't bother the white community on the other side of the tracks.

Elmo, who was ten years old at the time of his father's deeds, felt he carried the double burden of being a black person, and the son of a white man's killer all his life. In Crow, it was a sizable burden. He was a soldier during the latter part of World War II, and also served in the Korean Conflict. After leaving the Army, and returning to Crow, he managed to support his family by working for various farmers in the area until he fell from a hay truck, and broke his back. He recovered, but wasn't able to resume his farming work. The farmer had no Workers Compensation insurance; moreover, the farmer argued, Elmo Breed was an independent contractor, and he was not required to carry insurance on him.

Elmo moved his wife and three children into Crow. He applied for Social Security Disability, and obtained a monthly Government check to support his family; the inactivity made him quarrelsome, and he began drinking cheap wine to get through the day. His wife took the children, and moved to Tulsa where she had family. The youngest son, Fred, moved back in with his father, and Elmo curtailed his drinking to take care of this boy, the apple of his eye. When he was physically able, and the pain in his back was not too sharp, Elmo did some car mechanicing, and car trading. Fred Breed became a star tackle for the now-integrated Crow football team, and Elmo had high hopes for his son. The rejection by Southeastern was a bitter pill. Fred was now going to school at Langston University on a partial scholarship. Langston had been an all black university, but was now trying to present itself as just another university in the State of Oklahoma, although it remained predominantly black.

Elmo's disappointment stemmed from his belief that his son, to achieve any meaningful success, needed to live and work in the white man's world. Thus, when he did not get the bid from Southeastern, Elmo was sorely disappointed, and based on the coach's remarks about Joe Burk, blamed Burk. It was ironic that he was now helping Burk. His hatred for the white power structure overcame his personal animosity toward Burk, though, and he was willing to let the neighbors strike a blow at the ruling class in Crow. The poor and powerless frequently have an empathy that transcends race and personal hatreds, Elmo told himself.

Letha Mae pondered the problem with Elmo; she was almost certain Bugger had confided in him. *Fuck Elmo,* she thought, then giggled to herself. *Hell, yes, that's exactly what I'll do. I'll give old Elmo the best ride he has ever had, and he won't want to tell anybody anything. I wonder if black guys really do have bigger dicks?* She giggled again, looked at herself in the mirror, liked what she saw, and went off to get the boys ready—just like Elmo said. She laughed out loud.

CHAPTER 7

THE DAY CHOSEN FOR THE ROBBERY was the hottest day of the year, although the bandits could not have known beforehand, and it probably would have made little difference to Burk. He rarely concerned himself with the weather. The day was hot and sticky by ten a.m. Burk and Bugger parked the Ford in the alley, which ran between Payday Loan and the Indian shoe repair store on the north side of the alley. Burk knew the Choctaw Indian who ran the shoe repair store only as Ish, but had been there several times in his formative years to retrieve repaired shoes. Shoe repairs cost less than new shoes.

He determined they would have to keep the Ford running as he didn't want to execute his robbery plan, only to be thwarted by not being able to start the car afterwards. To confuse the victims, Burk determined he and Bugger would wear bulky jackets, and pantyhose pulled over their faces to distort their features.

His accomplice balked at wearing the pantyhose over his face when he tried it during a rehearsal, and found he had trouble breathing. He attempted to convince Burk and his sister that he could wear a bandana around his lower face, and not be recognized, similar to disguises in television Westerns, and he never recognized any of the bandits, he argued. Letha Mae persuaded him to tie a large scarf of hers around his lower face, and to wear an old straw hat someone left behind in the cafe. He also balked at putting the pistol in his front pants pocket underneath the bulky jacket, telling his conspirators that he knew a man who did that and the gun went off, and that fellow was not a full man anymore. Letha Mae wondered if her little brother had been experiencing some of life's pleasures, and was not telling her. She didn't press the issue after Burk showed her that her brother could stow his gun in the jacket pocket instead of his front pants pocket. Burk, without admitting to being persuaded by Bugger's tale about the man who was not a full man any more, decided to also carry his gun in the jacket pocket.

The inside of the car was an oven, and the two would-be robbers were the main course. *God, if Josie doesn't make her trek to the bank soon, we will be marinated in our own sweat,* Burk thought. When they first parked in the alley, Burk thought it would be good to alleviate any suspicion about a car running in the alley between businesses in the downtown area with two men sitting inside, that he would roll up the windows, and people would believe he and Bugger were sitting in their air conditioned car, enjoying a smoke. The car was not air conditioned, and thirty seconds of the intolerable heat without any breeze forced the abandonment of this deception.

He was surprised that he knew few people who passed by, and none of them paid any attention to the two men sitting in the alley with their car running, and sweat pouring down their faces. He realized the face of Crow was changing. National chain stores were moving into the area, and Weyerhaeuser, *the tree growing company*, brought some of their employees into the area when they purchased almost all of the timber in McCurtain County. Burk knew their money might be welcome, but no *born here* native would ever truly accept any of the newcomers. He had been told of the Goodyear manager being replaced when he remarked to the local newspaper that he had never seen so many people with missing teeth. The remark offended many of the locals, particularly the toothless genre.

Josie Williams strode into view, looked up the alley, appeared to change her mind, and walked out of sight heading toward the front entrance of the bank. Burk, who had watched her make this trip on several occasions, knew she could walk up the alley and enter the bank from the rear. The alternate route was to walk past the businesses on Main Street, turn right at the traffic light at Elm, and enter the bank's front door in the middle of the block. The would-be robber also knew that if she went into the bank from the rear after entering from the alley, she almost always returned the way she went. He didn't know why, but it proved to be true each time he watched her. Thus, he reasoned, she is going to return via the longer route, and will probably have the young bank vice-president with her. He also noted she usually had company when the longer route was taken. He hesitated, debating whether to tell Bugger it was almost certain Plan B would have to be utilized, and they would have to enter the loan company, hit it hard and fast, get the money, run back to the idling Ford, and head for Letha Mae.

Had Burk known what was happening in the lives of Josie and Dennis Banks, he may have re-thought his grand scheme. For, on this very day, Josie and Dennis were putting into operation a grand scheme of their own. Dennis had become acquainted with Rennie Morton, an eccentric, almost blind ninety-year-old woman, who maintained a safety deposit box at the bank. He inadvertently saw her retire a large amount of cash in her safety deposit box after unlocking the box for her, before leaving her alone in the room. His shoe had become untied, and he stooped to tie the shoe, could not grasp the lace, and dropped down on one knee to finish the job. The room seemed empty to the box owner, and she pulled a large amount of cash from her purse, and stuck the cash in her safety deposit box. The banker fled while she was putting the safety deposit box back in place.

Some inquiries turned up information that Rennie Morton flew to Las Vegas at intervals, and whenever she returned, she always visited the bank. An examination of the records of people using safety deposit boxes showed that, indeed, very punctually, on the third of every third month, Mrs. Morton called on the bank and her safety deposit box. Josie and Dennis determined that today would be the day they relieved Mrs. Morton of the riches she was keeping in her cache in the bank's vault. Dennis had a duplicate key of the bank's key, and he intended to pull a switch, and keep the dim sighted woman's key. The safety deposit box required the banker to insert his key, and then the customer insert her key, and, presto, the box would open. Because of her failing eyesight, she always let the bank employee insert her key too. Then, the employee would return her key, re-trieve the bank's key, and depart. No keys were needed to re-insert the box and shut the box; it was locked upon re-placement in its slot. Dennis simply intended to give her the bank's key, place hers in his pocket, and return the dupli-cate key he made to the bank's inventory.

He and Josie expected her to place her winnings or losings in the safety deposit box, re-insert the box, and leave, not being aware she had the bank's key, and not her own. Josie rented a safety deposit box after she and Dennis formulated the scheme. The plan provided for her to come to the bank, see Dennis to get her key, and both of them enter the vault. Instead of going to Josie's box, Dennis would take the cash from the Morton box, place it in her purse, and she would leave, much richer than when she walked in. If Ren-nie Morton ran true to form, no one would know anything was missing for three months, and, even then, Dennis rea-soned, the wealthy ninety-year-old might be reluctant to tell anyone. She had to know that hiding large amounts of cash in a safety deposit box was illegal, and telling could cause problems for her. In any event, both thieves intended to be many miles from the scene of the crime when, or if, it was reported. Brazil's lack of cooperation in extraditing Ameri-can fugitives appealed to the duet, and they expected to be moneyed citizens of South America.

Striding up Main Street, Josie wondered if Dennis would go through with the scheme. She knew he was vacil-lating, and being truthful with herself, did not blame him. After all, he was a vice-president in the local bank, well liked and respected. But when she found he had more ti-tle than income, and the bank was paying a member of the board of directors's son almost twice as much as Dennis for almost the same duties, she used this resentment to convince him the plan was foolproof. She knew he still entertained thoughts of staying in Crow. He argued that no one would know when the money was taken, and he was not the only one who ushered customers into the bank vault. There were two other officers, including the director's son. Making him examine the other two convinced Dennis that he would be the most likely suspect, and squelched his bid to remain in Crow. For Josie, her ambition was to see that her daughter was not raised in Crow, and that the child have a better life than she experienced. She knew the girl would always be known as the bastard child of Josie Williams as long as Josie remained in Crow, and resolved that was not going to happen if she had to rob Mrs. Morton herself.

Four years earlier, Josie's world seemed be perfect. She was easily the prettiest girl in Crow High School, and she knew it. She regularly admired herself in the mirrors at home, with and without clothes. The adoration of the teenage boys at school was a tonic to her, and she enjoyed making the shy ones more awkward than they already were; it was so easy. She also knew how a kind word from her made the day for some, and an unkind cut could devastate them. At times, the power was too much; she had to use it. But after she clubbed some awkward classmate with unkind words, she would have to spend extra time in the confessional booth at the local Catholic Church. During those times, she would rue her Catholic upbringing. Absolute guilt is necessary to be a Catholic, Josie thought; otherwise, the church could not exist, could not exert power over its followers.

With all her admirers, Josie had many chances at romance with boys in Crow, dated many, and had even gone steady with two young lads, but fervently hoped something better was waiting for her. She was totally unimpressed with all suitors through her junior year. Josie was a cheerleader for the second year, with grades to put her in competition for the top spot in her class. Many times she thought, *I may as well study; nothing in this high school is that interesting anyway, and it may be helpful later if I can figure out a way to go to college.*

Josie lived with her widowed mother who worked for the local propane company, and both knew the mother could not afford to send her to college. Josie's life changed forever when a new assistant coach was hired for the high school basketballers, and began attending the Catholic Church. His wife was also hired by the school board as an English teacher, but she chose to attend the Methodist Church instead of the Catholic Church.

Josie had a history class with the new coach, and enjoyed fantasizing about him with her friends. The unofficial poll among the female high schoolers was this young coach was the best hire during their tenure at Crow High School. With dark hair, *blue eyes to die for*, a ready smile, an athletic build, and personality pouring out of his pores, they considered him perfect. Josie saw him every Sunday at Mass and talked to him, but she knew he was married, and believed his interest was mere politeness—until the day she arrived early for his history class and eavesdropped on a conversation he was having with another coach, another new hire who was overweight and unpopular.

"I don't know how you stand it. All these young

pussies hanging on your every word, and ten to one, half would fuck your brains out if you just said the word," stated the unpopular one.

"Yeah. That's all I need. Getting fired from my first job because I can't keep my pants zipped. Besides, there's only one I would even consider, and she doesn't seem to have the hots for anybody," replied Scott.

"Yeah, which one you interested in, boy? I'll fix you up," leered his companion.

"I'm not interested in any of them, but if I were, Josie Williams would be the one I would want. Audrey Hepburn with tits. Hey, we better quit this; it's going to get us both in trouble," Scott stated. The class bell rang, and Josie didn't hear the reply of the second speaker. She wouldn't have cared anyway. Audrey Hepburn with tits. Wow, he had noticed her, and it wasn't just politeness.

Josie knew she shouldn't focus on this teacher, but the challenge was there. Besides, she knew she could have him now while the other girls just fantasized. Would it be worth it? There was only one way to find out. From that day forward, Josie used every excuse to touch Scott, to accidentally lay her breasts on his arm while talking to him, to lure him to sample her charms. And she saw it was working. She felt his eyes on her in class, in the hall, at church. She met his Methodist wife, and was totally unimpressed. One of her more intuitive classmates noticed, and told Josie that Mr. Black had the hots for her. Josie gave her a Mona Lisa smile, and defended Mr. Black, stating that he was just very nice, and anybody who believed otherwise just had a dirty mind. Josie knew where her mind was leading her, and occasionally became fearful because, in moments of sanity, she saw no future to the relationship.

The inevitable finally occurred after a basketball game coached by Scott. Josie led the cheers and volunteered to help him pick up trash on the school bus after everyone else went home. Both pretended to be very interested in the condition of the school bus until they came to the back seat. Scott looked at Josie in the skimpy cheerleader attire, bending over and picking up trash. She turned to face him, and in the dim light of the interior lights of the bus, she was the most beautiful female Scott had ever seen. In the back seat, Scott pulled Josie's cheerleader bottoms off, suckled the breasts, which put Audrey Hepburn to shame, and completed the act which both had been thinking about for some time.

Immediately afterward, he was contrite, asking Josie to forgive him, and then committed the error which eliminated any chance for a second go-round. He begged her to not tell his wife. Josie, looking at him with his pleading, anxious face, wondered why she ever pursued him. And the sex hadn't been that great, although his tongue on her nipples aroused her enough to forget the rough surface of the bus seat. She assured him she would not tell his wife, and also that the sex was history.

For him, it was a giant relief. Josie could still, at times, recall her amazement at how this wonderfully attractive man was concerned he would lose his cow of a wife. "*Love is strange,*" thought Josie. For her, problems were just beginning. Before school ended, Josie knew she was pregnant. Scott accepted a better coaching job in Western Oklahoma, and she never told him he was going to be a father. Abortion was not an option for this Catholic girl; she would not commit murder. She told her mother as soon as she knew she was pregnant, but refused to tell her who the identity of the father. She missed three days during her senior year to have her child, and graduated in the top ten percent of her class. She was removed from the National Honor Society, and extra-curricular activities were nil during her senior year.

Friends evaporated, except those who tried to deduce who the father of the child was. Bitterness and depression became her constant companions, and the only support came from her mother, and the local priest. Her mother and the priest attempted to convince her that life was not over, and better things lay ahead for a bright, beautiful girl like her. Josie accepted her fate by the time her beautiful child was born, but she was also determined to do whatever was necessary to leave this small town in her past. She did not want her daughter to achieve adulthood in Crow, Oklahoma. She was determined to find a way to avoid this fate. She considered the job with the loan company a stopgap measure. Although Josie knew she was paid more than most of the women in Crow, it was not enough.

CHAPTER

8

THE WAIT ON JOSIE to walk back in front of the idling Ford seemed an eternity to the sweating car sitters.

"There she is, but she's not by herself," Bugger proclaimed, watching Josie and Dennis walk by the alley.

"That's her boy friend," Burk taunted his companion. "The one I was telling you about. Wonder if they took an elevator ride today."

Bugger said nothing, looking morose. He hoped Josie would be alone, and when he told her to strip in the alley, she would recognize him and plead with him to take her along. Now, he was not looking forward to Plan B. Shortly after the couple passed the alley, Dennis appeared by himself, going back to the bank. It was time for Plan B.

When the two desperados burst into the loan company, Burk was pleasantly surprised. Only Wells and Josie appeared to be in the building. Josie was inserting the money into one of the cash drawers, and Wells was standing nearby. Sylvia did not appear to be in the building. The sweat and the pantyhose were blurring Burk 's vision, but he felt he could see well enough to accomplish his objective.

The sound of the door opening drew the attention of Josie and Wells to the front. Wells felt his legs turn to rubber bands when he saw the two men wearing face coverings and bulky jackets in the oppressive July heat. He often wondered what he would do if a robbery occurred at his loan company, and secretly hoped he would not be there if a robbery occurred. It hadn't been too long since that crazy guy and his girl friend robbed a loan company in Omaha, Nebraska, and killed all four people before leaving.

Josie felt a rush of adrenalin when the two burst through the door, but no real fear until the first man pulled a pistol out of his jacket pocket, and fired a bullet into the ceiling above her and Wells. Then, her stomach and kidneys appeared to be in combat with each other, reacting to the terror spread by the gunshot.

Migod, I'm going to piss on myself, she thought, then, with real effort, controlled her insides to keep this unpleasant event from occurring.

Burk, noting the abject fear he caused, felt an elation not felt since an almost perfect basketball game in his high school days. Whoo, this is wonderful! The adrenalin rush was greater than when the crowd burst into applause and cheering after a spectacular play. Then, calming himself, he pointed his pistol at Wells and Josie. Bugger stood behind him, and had not drawn his gun.

"Don't shoot! Don't shoot! You can have the money if that's what you want," Wells said. He had told both of his employees many times that the place was insured against such events, but never expected to have to follow his own advice. Now, all he wanted to do was to deliver the contents of the drawers to this crazy gunman, and get him out of there, preferably before he caused any harm to himself, or Josie.

Wells knew Sylvia was in the bathroom at the rear of the building, and hoped the large, black woman stayed there. He calculated fearfully that any heroics from her or anyone else could result in bullet holes in some place other than the ceiling. Wells looked at Bugger, and noted he did not seem to be armed, and was standing behind the smaller bandit, seemingly as intent on what the smaller robber was saying as he and Josie. He would later say that he wasn't even sure the larger bandit was with the small gunman, because he did not seem to be an active participant.

"Step away from those cash registers. Both of you, get in those booths, you in the first one, high pockets, and you in the second one, Josie," Burk said, calmly and in a tone one would use to direct traffic at a civic event. He was enjoying himself.

The "high pockets" designation caused Wells to pause, and attempt to examine the distorted features behind the pantyhose. He knew many of the town's citizenry made fun of the way he wore his pants belted several inches above his navel. The Chamber of Commerce even did a skit where an imitator buckled his belt across his chest, and walked across the stage, proclaiming himself to be the Great High Pockets Wells, the financier of the world. Wells enjoyed the parody as much as anyone in the audience. Now, he knew the gunman was a local.

High Pockets and Josie? Who was this guy? Similar thoughts were running through Josie's head. Neither was comforted by the thought that a local crazy was committing the crime. If anything, an out-of-towner might be less likely to cause harm. The area's propensity for violence was recognized by both victims.

"Git in there. Now!" Burk barked, his voice losing the civil tone. He pointed his pistol at Wells for emphasis. Wells looked at Josie, whose attention seemed to be riveted on the barrel of the gun. Josie could clearly see the bullets left in the chambers of the pistol, her mind focusing on the damage those missiles could do to her. The shine of the slugs caused an anxiety the gunman could not. Wells took her arm, and moved toward the booths where customers sat across a table in the small enclosures, pouring out their woes every day, explaining to Payday personnel why they needed money for bail bonds, school expenses, other loan companies, and a whole litany of problems which Payday was glad to help solve for an exorbitant interest rate.

When the two walked into the adjoining booths, Burk positioned himself where he could see both of them. Bugger had not moved from the front of the business. Burk now realized his accomplice's gun was still pocketed, and his only role thus far was being a front row spectator.

"Bu—. Hey, start getting the money out of those cash registers. I'll watch these two. Git with it. We cain't be here all day," Burk yelled at Bugger.

"God, I almost called him by name," Burk thought. "After I drilled him night and day to not use names, I almost did it myself." Seeing Bugger headed toward the cash registers, Burk turned his attention to the Payday staff.

"Take your clothes off, and throw them back to me. I mean all of them. NOW! DO IT," Burk shouted, looking back and forth to the two people ensconced in their booths.

"Why—" Wells started to question Burk. Burk raised the gun, sighted down the barrel at Wells' head. The dark shadow of death hovered over the Payday Loan company owner, causing him to immediately comply. His legs became more rubbery as he began unbuttoning his shirt. Josie followed his lead, and in short order, two piles of clothes appeared at the edge of the booths. Burk, standing nearer the booth of Wells, noticed Josie had not discarded her bra and panties.

"Everything, Miss Williams. I mean everything. Git those clothes off " Burk shouted.

Josie complied, then turned toward the wall, facing away. Burk, still excited by the events transpiring, could not help admiring the shapely woman in front of him. God, she had to have the most perfect ass he had ever seen.

"Brains! LOOK OUT!" Bugger's words jerked Burk's attention away from the nude female in front of him. He looked at Bugger who was pointing wildly at an area behind him. Burk turned just in time to catch the brunt of Sylvia Murdock's charge headon. Sylvia had watched the events unraveling from the farthest booth after exiting the bathroom, and awaited her opportunity to go into action. When Burk was distracted by Josie's final disrobing, she decided the time to act presented itself. The contact knocked Burk on his back, propelling him to a landing spot near Josie's booth. The back of his head landed on her purse, saving him a massive headache later, and from a likely concussion. The black woman grinned at the sight of the bandit stretched out in front of her. She should have watched Bugger.

Forgetting that he had a gun in his pocket, Bugger ran headlong toward Burk's attacker, catching her in a driving tackle with his head in her chest and his arms wrapped around her; it would have made his eighth grade coach proud. Sylvia, concentrating on Burk, did not see Bugger until it was too late to attempt evasive action. She saw Bugger putting the money into his jacket pockets, but her assessment of the two led her to believe he was the least dangerous. He displayed no gun, and did not seem to be enthusiastic about what was happening. She miscalculated his loyalty, and his speed. The impetus of Bugger's charge carried him and the large woman past the booth Wells was in, and ended with Sylvia hitting the floor on her back with Bugger on top of her. Her head hit the hard floor, and consciousness dimmed. She moaned, trying to re-energize herself, then lay inert.

Burk sprang to his feet, training the pistol on Wells first, then on Josie. He looked down at the purse by his feet, noting the catch holding it closed, had sprung open, revealing a large mass of money inside. Burk paused, not comprehending what he was seeing. God, there was more money in that purse than Bugger had stuffed in his pockets from the cash registers.

"Good Lord," thought Burk. "The mother lode is in that purse, not in those cash registers." He grabbed the purse.

Looking back over her shoulder, Josie, who was still facing away from the action, saw Burk eyeing the fortune stashed in her purse. She hadn't taken time to count it, but knew it was at least $100,000 wrapped in packets. Forgetting her modesty, she turned and faced Burk.

"Leave my purse alone, you son-of-a-bitch. You've got what you came for. Now, get out of here and leave us alone," she said forcefully, trying to look as stem as she could in her natural state.

Burk, unswayed now by the luscious female form in full view in front of him, snapped the purse shut and put it under his arm.

"Shut your mouth, you whore, or I'll shut it for you permanently," Burk said, pointing the gun and stepping forward until he was a scant two feet from the nude employee. The cartridges loomed large again to Josie, and she quelled. She did not doubt he would shoot her.

"Brains, you promised she wouldn't get hurt. She don't mean nothin'. Don't shoot her. Lets get out of here," Bugger pleaded, walking away from the black woman lying on the floor, and toward Burk. Bugger was attempting to administer aid to Sylvia when he noted the confrontation between his partner and Josie. His concern for Josie overrode his concern for Sylvia. There was still a scant hope that Josie would recognize him and want to run away with him.

"Goddamit! I ain't going to shoot your girl friend. Not if l don't have to. Let's go. You first," Burk said, gesturing toward the door.

Wells' mind was whirling. Brains, your girl friend, the smaller robber 's sudden interest in Josie's purse. What in God's name was happening? The rubber bands in his legs were changing to steel bands and he was becoming angry more than frightened. He decided he wasn't going to let these two-bit punks come into his place, rob him, and humiliate him and his employees. He placed a foot backward to push off, and rushed Burk.

Noting the placement of the foot to begin the rush, Burk swung the gun forward, and started to warn Wells again when Wells took a second step, and launched himself toward Burk. Stepping back, Burk brought the pistol barrel down hard on Wells' forehead. The force of the blow caused his trigger finger to tighten, and the gun exploded. The bullet went through the ceiling, and into the roof. Wells' knees buckled, blood poured from the split in his forehead, and he crumpled to the floor.

Bugger had started toward the door, did not see Wells being hit in the forehead, but heard the shot, and saw Wells in a crumpled heap on the floor.

"Oh, God, you have killed him," Bugger whimpered. "Now, they'll kill us. I'm gittin' out of here. I don't want nothin' more to do with this."

He turned, and ran out the front door, turning left outside the door and away from the alley where the 1957 Ford was still running.

"WAIT! Wait, you fool," Burk implored, knowing Bugger intended to run all the way home and there was nothing he could do to stop him. Quickly, he assessed the damage in the loan company. Sylvia Murdock was attempting to pull herself to a sitting position, Wells was moving his hand toward his bloody forehead, and Josie was mesmerized by him and her purse, her eyes alternating from his blurred features behind the pantyhose, and his grip on the purse. She was, at present, the only danger to his escape.

"I'm leaving now. No one's dead yet, but you will be first if you try to follow me. Stay in that booth, put your clothes on, and then you can call the police, your sweetheart, your mother, or Dial-a- Prayer. But don't try to follow me," Burk stated to Josie, emphasizing his last instruction. Keeping the gun pointed at her, he backed toward the door. When he reached the door, he jerked it open, ran to the right, and headed toward the Ford in the alley.

Josie examined the sights around her. Wells, still unclad, was trying to stem the flow of blood from his head, but the dark red liquid was spilling through his fingers onto the floor. Sylvia was sitting, but appeared to be having trouble trying to stand. Josie heard tires squeal, a motor raced to its fullest pitch, and knew the robber reached his car and was beginning his escape. In the recesses of her mind, she remembered the old car sitting in the alley when she started her trip to the bank. God, that's our money! He's getting away with our money! She grabbed her skirt, put it in front of her, and ran out the door without any plan except to do whatever she could to retrieve her dream, the dream leaving at full throttle in the old brown Ford.

Burk had ran up the alley, opened the door on the driver's side of the Ford, put the gun back in the jacket pocket, threw the purse in, and jumped behind the steering wheel. He was panicking. The inadvertent shot into the ceiling disconcerted him, almost as much as it had his partner. He pulled the gear shift lever down into drive, floored the gas pedal and headed toward Main Street.

The alley sloped down at almost thirty degrees before emptying onto Main. When the car hit the dip before entering Main Street, Burk turned sharply to the right. The speed and the angle were too much, and the Ford flipped, landing on its top, and careening into the middle of the thoroughfare. Burk was thrown about in the upside down car like a pinball in one of the favorite pastimes at Sam's Drive-in. His head hit the top of the car, and then the doorpost. His arm became locked in the steering wheel, and felt like it was being torn from its socket. His ankle banged against the dash, causing incredible pain, making his eyes water under the pantyhose mask. But, when the car stopped spinning, Burk realized that despite his pains, he survived the mishap.

With the windows down, he suffered no cuts. The purse was sitting on his face and his mind was reeling. He had to get out of the car. The roof of the vehicle was almost flattened on the driver's side. He tried the driver's door, and found he could not open it. After placing the purse in front of him, he forced himself through the window opening, using his elbows to drag his bruised body out of the car. Three men began converging on the car from different directions.

"Watch out! He's got a gun. He'll shoot you. He's already killed Mr. Wells," Josie shrieked at the men headed toward the car, trying to hold her skirt where it would cover her breasts and vagina. The men, seeing her, now stopped, uncertain about what they should do.

Burk, hearing her, looked back into the car for the gun. It didn't appear to be in the car. He grabbed the purse and stood up, looking around and assessing the terrain. Josie, seeing the men stop, viewed the purse and determined to protect her dream.

Still holding the skirt in front of her, she ran toward Burk. He saw the naked woman headed full tilt toward him, and braced himself. He was being pummeled more by crazy women today than he had ever been beaten by men.

Josie launched herself at the purse when she was two feet away, grabbing it with both hands and pulling it to the pavement, scraping her knees and elbows when she hit the pavement. The snap of the purse released, and two packets of the money spilled out; Josie grabbed the loose packets with one hand, and held the purse against her stomach with the other hand.

Surprised by her snatching of the purse, Burk looked down at her, lying on the purse, with the perfect ass he admired such a short time before bared for all of Crow to see. Although there were only a handful of people near enough to see Josie, at least a dozen men claimed to have seen her in the raw when this event was discussed at the various gathering places shortly after the event. The three men who were there were torn between looking at her, and taking action against Burk. People were coming out of other stores, and traffic had stopped on Main Street. Burk reacted swiftly, the purse being as important to him as it was to Josie. He bent down, reached under the woman and grabbed the purse. Josie, feeling the purse being pulled, scrambled to her feet, still holding on to the purse. The skirt dropped to the pavement as she lost all interest in modesty; she intended to keep the purse, at all costs. She held the two packets in one hand, with that hand placed across the top of the purse, and cradled the purse in the crook of her other arm.

Burk pulled, and being stronger than Josie, ripped the purse from her grasp. Josie, blood streaming down her elbows and knees, kicked at him. Seeing her dream evaporate in the heat in the center of Main Street, she screamed, "Help me! Help me!"

One of the men converging on the combatants decided he had seen enough. He would help this naked, bleeding woman who was waging war with a masked man over her purse.

"Look out, Jim. He's got a gun, and he's already killed Don Wells," an onlooker shouted, seeing a new fighter was going to join in the fray. The new fighter hesitated. Burk then remembered he had placed the gun in the jacket before getting into the car. He pulled the gun, fired it into the air and the would-be heroes backed away.

Looking at the crowd of people gathering, Burk decided discretion was the better part of valor. The center of Main Street with the upside down Ford was still clear. Burk put on a burst of speed, running through the attempted grab by a citizen who arrived at the scene of the commotion.

"Somebody call the police. He's getting away," shouted a woman who just arrived.

"I'll git my gun from my pickup. I'll git that son-of-a-bitch," yelled the man who was determined to help Josie. Burk, running hard on an ankle that was shooting pain on every step, gained new impetus from this last threat. He was well aware that a rifle in a rack in a pickup was more common than not in this part of Oklahoma.

"Someone get something to cover that poor woman, and something for her knees and elbows," the newly arrived female stated, looking at a distraught Josie who was still clutching the two loose packets of dollars, while watching Burk flee. Hearing the comments by the sympathetic female, Josie teared up, her shoulders shaking with sobs. She picked up her skirt, placed it in front of her, with the money clutched close to her stomach.

"Stop him. He's got my money," Josie wailed to the confused bystanders. Noting Burk's burst of speed when he sprinted down the main thoroughfare, Josie knew her chances of catching him, sans clothes or not, were slim and nil. The comforting onlooker put her arms around her, and began walking her to the loan company office. One man chased Burk for a short distance then stopped. The rifle owner was still trying to get his weapon out of the rack. The other onlookers had their eyes trained on Josie.

Burk could feel blood coming out of his nose as he ran, and breathing was becoming a real problem behind the pantyhose mask. He knew it was approximately one and one-half miles to where Letha Mae was waiting because he measured it on her odometer, but felt if he didn't run all out now, the man getting the gun from the pickup would drop him before he saw Letha Mae. Driving a car to her location would have taken scant time, but he did not have that luxury. Also, if he continued running down Main Street, he knew he would run past the sheriff s office, and the county courthouse. Although it was likely that everyone was inside to escape the heat, he could not take that chance.

When he covered the two blocks immediately before entering the courthouse block, he turned right, went midway down the street, and ran into the alley behind the courthouse. His breathing was becoming ragged, and he felt the pantyhose filling with his blood. He stopped on entering the alley and ripped the pantyhose mask off. Relief was instantaneous. He threw the mask down, and looked behind him. No pursuer was in sight. The wicked flee when no one pursues, Burk thought, remembering one of the few Biblical phrases he knew.

He felt his nose; it was wet, but the bleeding appeared to have stopped. He gazed at the pantyhose mask in his hand, and then looked around for a place to get rid of it and spotted a dumpster sitting beside a small metal building. He recognized the building; it was a storage shed for tools used by jailhouse trustees for maintaining the lawn, and other similar work around the courthouse. It appeared to be locked, but Burk, having retrieved tools from this building while awaiting his trial for cattle thievery, remembered that the deputies usually just placed the lock in a position where the building appeared to be locked, but usually was not. Their reasoning was that few Crow residents would want to steal tools that would then require them to perform manual labor.

Burk checked the lock, and found that indeed, the building was not locked. He threw the pantyhose mask and his gloves into the dumpster, and entered the building. An almost unbearable wave of heat hit him in the face when he stepped in, causing him to experience a sense of vertigo. Gritting his teeth, Burk plunged deeper into his second oven of the day. He stepped to the north wall where a peephole allowed him to see the parking lot at the back of the courthouse. He saw two of the sheriffs deputies cars were still in the parking lot. He didn't have long to wait. Two deputies came running out of the back door, putting on hats and holding onto their guns. Each of the deputies got into a different car, and hastened out of the parking lot. Burk calculated the sheriff had been notified a robbery had taken place, and the deputies were headed in the direction given by witnesses.

Although the heat was making his temples throb, and he felt himself becoming dizzier, Burk forced himself to wait to be sure no other law enforcement types were coming out the back door of the courthouse. Then, he took off the jacket, wrapped the purse in it, and stepped out into one hundred degree heat, which felt like an arctic blast after being inside the metal building.

He was shirtless, but he knew a shirtless man in the middle of the summer was not an uncommon sight. Seeing no policemen, sheriffs deputies, nor anyone else in the alley, he took off at a lope past the courthouse rear doors. He knew this alley, knew it would take him past the funeral home, then a jog over to the next street, then three blocks to where Letha Mae awaited—at least he hoped she was still waiting there. God, I should have prepared a contingency plan, he thought, as he loped past the funeral home. When he turned right to take the jog over to the next street, he looked both ways with real apprehension, but saw no one. The heat was keeping the townspeople in, and the police were evidently looking in the wrong place. *Good,* Burk thought, slowing some. *I've got to conserve my energy; I've still got a way to go.* Thinking while running, he determined that he could not leave the rendezvous point with Letha Mae and the boys.

Steven Parker

CHAPTER 9

LETHA MAE AND THE TWO BOYS were waiting in the grassy area beside the Second Baptist Church. A slide and swings had been erected for children, and the boys were swinging, stirring whatever breeze they could to keep from burning up in the heat. Letha Mae was leaning on the hood of the Maverick, watching the boys, and hoping to see a 1957 Ford with Burk and Bugger turning off Main, and coming down the road to the church.

Burk's plan was to leave the 1957 Ford in an area immediately behind the church, a pseudo alley with a cloth door which could be lowered to enclose any car parked there, and to keep the car from being seen from the street. He speculated the minister built the contraption to keep his car from being unbearably hot on Sunday morning after services were over. He used the hiding place one night when the local police were chasing him, and found it effective on that occasion. Burk believed it would be effective in eluding the police again, and would also keep the stolen car from being found until the following Sunday when the preacher would discover it.

Letha Mae had no misgivings about using the church as a getaway place, but rehearsed what she would say if anyone stopped and asked what she and the boys were doing playing on these swings when Garfield Elementary school was only a block away, and their swings were in the shade. She didn't like any of the ploys she dreamed up, and decided to be as rude as possible to anyone who dared ask what they were doing there; then, maybe, they would leave, and everything would be all right. She looked in the other direction and saw Burk jogging with something in his arm.

He was shirtless, and covered with sweat. She admired his easy gait and his body as he neared her, but felt almost physical agony as she realized something must have gone wrong for him to be coming like this. Where was Bugger? Where was the car? Why was Joe alone, and running? Noticing he was not running like someone was chasing him, Letha Mae calmed some, but her anxieties spiraled upward as she noted the blood on his face.

"Oh, God, Joe. What happened? Are you alright? Where's Luther?" the words spilled out of Letha Mae as she ran to meet her partner in crime.

Burk stopped. "Don't touch me. You'll get dirty and sweaty, and you might have to explain why. Take this jacket and purse. There's more money than we ever thought. Go home. Wait for me or my phone call.

Bugger is not hurt, but he may be caught. If there are any police cars at your house, do not go home. I am going to Sam's Drive in. I'll call your house. If you are there, and the police are also there, tell me my uncle is alright, he did not die. If the police are not there, and you don't expect them, just tell me to come on home. I'm going to take one pack of these bills so I'll have it to run on if things don't work out. If I call your house, and don't get an answer at all, I will know you have taken the money and headed for Mexico. Wait for me at the Mexican border for as long as you can," Burk blurted, winded after the long speech and his run.

"Oh, Joe, I'll wait forever. You know that. You know I love you," Letha Mae said, then realized she had spoken the truth; she did love him.

Burk seemed bewildered by his paramour's burst of raw emotion. He didn't know how to respond, but knew she was sincere. For the first time since they had been together, Letha Mae noted a look of confusion on Burk's face. He always seemed so sure of himself before. She didn't know of Burk's concern about losing her, and now he had no idea what he was supposed to do about this woman declaring her love for him. Few people had loved Burk in his lifetime, and none had told him they did, excepting females caught up in the excitement of the sex act. Burk noted their love ended as soon as it began. *We don't have time to have this kind of conversation,* he thought.

Letha Mae wailed, on the verge of tears, *Where's Luther? You know I can't leave him. What happened?* She knew she would never forgive herself if her brother was hurt. For some reason, she never considered he might be hurt during the robbery. Now, seeing the blood on Burk, and knowing things didn't go as planned, she imagined her poor simple minded brother shot, or worse, pursued by law enforcement and dogs, and scared to death.

Burk was relieved to deal with this subject as opposed to having to sort out his and Letha Mae's feelings for each other.

"God, Letha Mae, I don't know what happened to Bugger. He left running toward your house. He's probably there, watching cartoons. I can't stay," Burk said, turning and striding toward Garfield Elementary School. He hesitated, looked at Letha Mae as if he were going to say something, changed his mind, and began running. This was not a time to have a meaningful conversation.

CHAPTER

10

BUGGER HAD, INDEED, GONE HOME. After leaving the loan company, he didn't break stride until he turned into his home yard approximately one and one half miles from the loan company. He discarded his face covering, and the hat in the first block, but kept the jacket filled with Payday cash for the entire distance. People who saw him wondered what a man wearing a jacket in July was doing running as if he were in a race. One of the observers told police later that he thought it was a new way to lose weight, i.e., put on a jacket, run in hundred degree heat and sweat off the pounds.

After arriving home, Bugger could not decide what to do. He knew Letha Mae was waiting at Second Baptist Church, but he wasn't sure if he could find the church. He was afraid Burk might be coming after him with a gun. God, he didn't have to kill Mr. Wells. Now they'll think I helped him do it, and they'll put me in the electric chair too. I'll turn myself in, and maybe they won't put me in the electric chair. Bugger saw a movie where the actor, James Cagney died in the electric chair, and he was certain he didn't want that fate. He started to go back out the front door of the house when Elmo appeared on the porch. Bugger was relieved. If anyone could help him, it was Elmo.

CHAPTER

11

BURK WENT TO SCHOOL at Garfield Elementary many years before, and knew he could enter a pasture behind the school, go through the pasture, continue past the electric transformer in the next pasture, enter the woods where a creek ran parallel to the old highway that ran from Crow to Burlington. His plan was to enter these woods, wade the creek to throw off any dogs which they may have obtained to track him, and leave the creek when he reached a point in the woods which was perpendicular to Sam's Drive-In on Highway Seventy.

He would have to cross the highway, and enter more woods which ran all the way to back of Sam's Drive-In, but he calculated that unless the law enforcement people had become more efficient in recent years, he would be at Sam's before anyone thought of getting dogs, and would be out of Sam's before they actually deployed the dogs.

Burk also knew the woods of southeastern-Oklahoma

were notorious as hiding places for fugitives. When he was a small child, a lawbreaker became involved in a gunfight with deputies near Burlington, scarcely twelve miles away, and after killing them, went into the forests north of Burlington. (This was before Weyerhaeuser clear-cut these forests.) Two weeks of intense manhunting did not result in the capture of this fugitive; but one of the deputies managed to shoot him in the dick, and his swollen member caused him to turn himself in to seek medical help.

Rex Brinlee, the infamous Tahlequah murderer escaped from Big Mac earlier that summer, and lawmen were unable to flush him out of hiding. Ticks and chiggers, however, caused the infamous criminal to seek his prison bunk after two weeks in the woods near Eufaula, almost one hundred-fifty miles north, and almost out of Little Dixie. The notorious killer sought a deputy where he could return to prison and be treated for the hundreds of tick and chigger bites inflicted in his two-week vacation. And Burk knew those ticks and chiggers are amateurish compared to the ticks and chiggers down here.

The banged up robber was not worrying about ticks and chiggers, though. He did not intend to spend many minutes in these flatland woods. His ankle was throbbing, his right eye continued to water, and his arm ached, but he was able to maintain a steady pace through the pastures until he reached the creek. He spent days with other boys jumping into and out of this creek when he was younger. At some of the wider places, he fell in when he didn't make the jump. He had been chastised and paddled by Mrs. Brown, the Garfield principal, on several occasions for leaving the school grounds and playing in the creek.

Now, he was glad he knew this little creek, and all of its twists and turns.

When he reached the creek, he knelt down, washed his face, and head, and then submerged his head under the water. The water felt wonderful. Burk noted the creek was full, reinforcing the Crow Gazette's story that this was the wettest year the locality had experienced for some time. The newspaper reported the county received more than twenty-nine inches for the first six months, at least six inches more than usual. Six people were struck by lightning in a recent storm, according to the newspaper. Burk felt like one of the six unfortunates.

For the first time, he realized his face was swollen on the left side. It must have happened in the car wreck, he reflected. He was lucky that he was not hurt worse. Maybe fate would be better to him than it had been in the past, although Burk did not feel he had been ill treated by the world. He told listeners that his philosophy was you made your own luck. He claimed religion did not play a large part in his dreams and schemes. He had seen too many inmates acquire a love of Jesus Christ immediately before parole hearings, and revert to their old ways after being turned down. Burk told everyone he subscribed to a theory he read in the prison library, claiming the first divine was the first rogue who met the first fool.

The truth of the matter was, Burk presented as false an image as the pre-parole inmates who embraced Christianity for a very short time to obtain parole, but in a different way. Contrary to the philosophical nonsense he spouted, he was a praying man, and had been all his life. He negotiated everything with a God he recognized, but did not claim to understand. He had an insurmountable problem in visualizing this supreme being as "Our Father in Heaven" because he had almost no contact with any male he could visualize as being godly. He worried that people would think he was completely bonkers when he told them the face he saw as God's was his own.

In high school, in his negotiations with this God, he offered good behavior for touchdowns, basketball scores, baseball hits, and test scores. In prison, he prayed every night just for endurance to see him through his sentence. His offer in prison was never to steal again.

Right now, as he waded in the creek, he was offering to never steal anything again if he could just get away with this theft. He reasoned with his deity that his thievery—the cattle and now the loan robbery—were isolated incidents, and if things would just begin to go right with this escape, he would never, ever steal again. After all, two events of thievery were not much in the overall scheme of life, he implored, and surely God could overlook this event. He rationalized away all the candy bars, cigarettes, soda pops, and other small items he shoplifted over the years as too trivial to fit into the grand scheme of life. He looked upward, as if God were sitting on one of the fleecy clouds above listening to him. He turned off these thoughts when he visualized himself on one of the clouds. This has got to be sacrilegious, he argued with himself.

His bargain offered, and—he hoped—accepted, he reasoned that he had no choice but to keep going. His mind flashed back to a recurring dream he experienced as a child. In this dream, he was a fugitive being chased naked down the Main Street of Crow while people threw stones at him. *At least, I'm not naked, and no one even knows where I am,* he thought.

When he reached an area of the creek that he felt was nearly perpendicular to Sam Stone's Drive-In on Highway Seventy, he exited the creek. He knew he would have to cross a short area of pasture, cross an old highway, re-enter woods, and travel another mile before reaching the business.

Burk looked both ways down the old highway before running across. It had been the main road between Crow and Burlington many years ago. It crossed Little River approximately two miles from where Burk now crossed over, winding its way down Nigger Hill. This was the Nigger Hill that, according to local legend was so named because a black man was lynched there, and his body buried in the road. This was the blacktop Burk trod many times going to the river to swim, wondering if he was walking on the black man's grave.

He entered the woods on the other side, and ran far enough into the woods where he felt he could not be seen by traffic on the highway, then slowed to a walk. He was becoming winded, and all of his aches and pains seemed to be magnified by the heat in the woods. His tennis shoes squished from his wade in the creek. *At least I'm in the shade,* Burk thought, as he walked past a pond he remembered from days past. Moments later, he saw the rear of Sam's Drive-In, and was gladdened that his memory of the geography from his early years was accurate. He paused to catch his breath, and decide how to approach Sam.

Steven Parker

ELMO PERCEIVED Bugger was distraught to the point where he might do something to harm himself or someone else and said, "Calm down. Calm down. Nothin's ever as bad as you think it is," Elmo said, placing his hand on Bugger's shoulder.

"Oh, God, Elmo, it's worse. Joe killed Mr. Wells, and they're going to kill him and me too. I didn't want to do this in the first place. I'm going to give back their money. Do you think they'll let me go if I tell them Joe did it," Bugger sobbed. "And I didn't think up any of this. All this Plan A and Plan B stuff was Joe too. I was lying to you before. I never planned any of this."

Should I tell him he need not worry that anyone is ever going to accuse him of planning anything, and I never believed he was the planner even when he was the most proud of the plans he considered brilliant. Elmo, as Burk suspected, had been privy to the chicanery being planned next door from the beginning. His dislike for Wells and the white power structure in Crow kept him silent, and indeed, he hoped Burk could succeed, but harbored serious doubts about any criminal who would take Bugger as a partner.

"No one is dead," Elmo assure him. "Wells is probably resting comfortably in the hospital. Your friend split his head, and Josie Williams has skinned knees and elbows, but she's gonna be alright," the neighbor told Bugger, keeping his hand on his shoulder, trying to calm him. Elmo didn't know if it was the none dead announcement or the report on Josie Williams, but Bugger seemed to relax. Then he tensed again.

"You're just telling me that. How do you know? What about that nigger woman?" Bugger questioned, belligerently. Briefly, Elmo was offended and angered by the "nigger woman" reference, but he considered the source, and realized Bugger would not even understand why he was angry. He was simply repeating what his peers would have said, although the few who knew better would not have said it to Elmo.

"Those fools have been talking their head off on the scanner. They're looking for Burk in the area by the sale barn," Elmo said deliberately, trying to determine if Bugger had any idea where Burk was.

Burk would have been gratified by this statement. The sale barn was in the opposite direction, and miles away from Sam's Bar and Drive-In.

When he made the turn to go into the alley behind the courthouse, a chaser speculated to the policeman that he ran toward the high school, lying to the policeman about his proximity to Burk when he spied him "running dead out" toward the high school. The chaser could see his name in the newspaper the next day as the hero who guided law enforcement to the location of the bandit, and was not overly concerned that he might be leading law enforcement astray.

"Just simmer down. This thing may still work out. Yo' partner is tough as a boot, and he's no dummy. They ain't caught him yet. I think you're in the best place yo' could be. Is anybody following you?" Elmo asked, then walked to the front door to see if he could see any activity on the gravel road.

The road contained no dust devils, visible heat waves arose from the middle, but the road appeared to be abandoned. The heat and humidity did not inspire walks down dusty roads at midday. Elmo started to return to Bugger when he spotted a car coming, stirring up the white dust. It was a familiar car; Elmo recognized it as Letha Mae's.

Steven Parker

CHAPTER

13

BURK HITCHED UP HIS PANTS, and strode toward the back door of Sam's. He noted a shallow ditch had been dug behind the drive-in bar, exposing the sewer pipe. Some kind of plumbing problem, he considered. No one appeared to be at the business, but Burk knew Sam usually arrived around noon, or shortly before, to check on the food and beer stock, and to insure all of the machines would be ready for the evening crowd. At times, he had employees arrive early to help him, and, at other times, he was alone. Burk spotted Sam's Cadillac in the shade of the building, and guessed he was alone. He knocked on the back door, then tested it to see if it was locked. It wasn't. Burk pulled the door open, and stepped inside.

"Sam, you in here? It's Joe Burk. Can I come in?" Burk queried in a voice he hoped was loud enough to be heard, but not so loud to be threatening. He was afraid Sam might shoot first, and ask questions later.

"I see you. What the hell do you want?" Burk heard the voice come from an area to his right, which was not well lighted. He recognized the voice as Sam's.

"Not much. Maybe just the use of your telephone. I'll pay for it," Burk said, trying to see if Sam was covering him with his gun. Maybe this wasn't such a good idea after all. Sam knew him from the drive-in, and had talked with him many times, but Burk, like most of the bar patrons, never knew exactly what Sam was thinking. He thought Sam admired his fighting prowess, but, again, you could never be sure about Sam. He might just shoot, and claim Burk was burglarizing him. Burk heard another voice, then static. Was someone with Sam? He heard more static, then another voice telling someone they needed dogs near the sale barn, and all law enforcement were to converge there immediately. It was a police scanner. God, they were looking for him all the way over on the other highway. Burk smiled, and almost laughed.

"Makes you happy, does it?" Sam said, walking into the light. He was, as Burk had surmised, carrying a pistol in his right hand. Burk was relieved to see it was not pointing at him.

"So you robbed ol' high pockets, and split his head. Boy, I thought you didn't like prison. Do you think they're going to give you a medal? How many chances do you think you're going to get in a lifetime?" Sam inquired, looking almost sadly at Burk, at his swollen face, skinned elbow, and wet feet. Burk looked out the back door, not knowing how to respond.

"Who do you want to call? You better call 'em, and catch a fast horse out of town. They won't be looking for you on the other side of town too long. The way you look, somebody is bound to have spotted you, or your accomplice. What dunderhead did you rope into this harebrained scheme with you? No, don't tell me. Just make your call, get you a ride, and get out." Sam finished his speech with a point of the gun to the outside.

The crunch of tires on the gravel parking lot drew both men's attention to the front of the drive-in. A sheriff's cruiser with two deputies slowed to a stop near the front door. The car doors swung open, and two large men exited from opposite sides of the car at the same time. The deputies were Trace Moore and Ronnie Smith. Burk and Sam knew them, and for the most part, did not have anything against them. Recently, a prisoner who escaped from these two drowned in Little River when the current swept him downstream. There was speculation about the *escape* since the would-be swimmer was dating Moore's sister, and it was generally known that Moore did not approve of the match. Burk debated his chances on a headlong flight out the back door, and back into the woods.

"Don't even think it. You wouldn't get a chance to swim Little River," Sam said, then grinned as if he knew a joke, and no one else had caught on yet.

"Get out there, and get in that ditch. You just became the man I hired to help me fix this sewer line," Sam said, gesturing toward the open ditch. A shovel leaned against the side of the ditch. Burk grasped Sam's plan, and started to question the wisdom of the same, then realized he was a man without many options. He hastened out the back door and was in the ditch shoveling when the deputies entered the front door after knocking.

"Sam, what's goin' on? You getting ready for a big night?" Moore said, walking into the bar. "Hello, Sam," Smith said, following Moore, and scanning the bar for patrons, bugs, mice, or whatever he could see. "You alone?"

"Hell no. I've got Marilyn Monroe in here. What do you care whether I'm alone or not? What do you want?" Sam asked in a neutral tone. If he could just turn them around before they even saw Burk, it would be better for him and Burk. He asked himself, *How far do I go with this help before I start protecting myself. Why,* he wondered to himself, *didn't I just let that boy run out the door, and watch the target practice?*

"Well, Sam, if you've got Marilyn Monroe in here, you must like corpses. She's been dead for a long time now," Moore said, amicably, continuing to walk around the bar.

"I've been a necrophiliac for a long time now. Didn't you know?" Sam said it with a smile, thinking to himself, *Let these suckers figure that one out.*

"Necro—what? What did you say you were?" Moore said. Sam grinned wider.

"It means he likes to fuck corpses," said Smith. "Cut the shit, Sam. I know you've got a scanner, and I know you know we're looking for a robber. Have you seen anybody out this way that might fit his description?" Smith said, amused by the word game the bar owner was having with his big, dumb partner. He stepped in front of Sam to convey this was serious business. Sam was mildly astonished. A deputy with a vocabulary. Having seen many police reports, Sam didn't believe there were many of the local law enforcement troop who could put a subject and a verb together, much less define words with more than two syllables. He didn't know

Smith well, but made a mental note to himself to watch him more carefully in the future. Right now, he had a decision to make. Was it going to be Sam, the businessman, or Sam, the friend? Or something else?

"I've been here for about two hours, setting up for to-night. I've got a man out back digging a ditch so I can have plumbing tonight. Why aren't you boys helping with the search out at the sale barn?" Sam said, appearing to be only mildly interested in the robbery and search.

"You've got a man digging a ditch in this God awful heat. That son-of-a-bitch must be desperate for a job. Who is it?" Moore said, moving toward the back of the building, and peering out of the back window.

"God, come here, Ronnie. It's Joe Burk. How the mighty have fallen." Moore said, resting his hands on his hips, and watching Burk broiling in the sun while pitching dirt from the shallow ditch.

Burk, meanwhile, was thinking, "I must really be crazy. Three times already today I've been in places hotter than Hell on Judgment Day, and Sam Stone is getting free labor, and turning me in at the same time. Ol' Sam and them deputies are probably slapping their thighs with laughter, watching me sweating in this miserable, stinking hole. Well, the only consolation is that I damn well know he didn't plan it." Burk actually smiled at his plight. Maybe this would be the time to ask Sam about his picture being in his dead mother's mementos.

"Jesus, I think the son-of-a-bitch has gone nuts in this heat. He's smiling, looks as happy as a hog in a knee deep wallow," Smith said, a tinge of envy in his voice.

"He may be crazy now, but he was a hell of a football

player when he played here. I used to go watch him every Friday night," Moore said, watching the smaller man's back muscles moving with the thrusting of the shovel. "What the hell happened to his face, Sam?"

"He told me he got in a fight with that Dierks bunch at the Hoot and Holler last night. Looks like they worked him over pretty good," Sam lied. He knew, however, that a small gang from Dierks, Arkansas, had been hitting the local bars lately, and challenging all comers. Two of the Arkansas boys were arrested the previous week.

"Well, I wish to hell somebody would whip their ass good, and send them back across the line for good. They're sure as hell troublemakers," Smith said. He started to add that he knew the two who spent the night in the local jail would not be among the next wave to come across the state line; he and Moore convinced those two boys that they did not want to be Arkansas Travelers. He had not been in the area long, however, and he wasn't sure how this bar owner would react to any tales about the treatment of prisoners.

"He must have played without his helmet," Smith continued. "Anyone working in this heat, and enjoying it, can't be playing with a full deck," Moore snorted.

"That's funny. I saw ol' Joe score the winning touchdown against Burlington without his helmet. He hit the line goin' full blast, and they tore his helmet off, but didn't get him down. The next thing they knew, he was tearing down the sideline, bareheaded, all the way to the end zone." Moore told the story with enthusiasm. "I hate to see him in this shape. He coulda done better. He really didn't have much of a chance. His old mother couldn't stay off the sauce, and Burk really had it rough."

"Leave his mother out of this. She did the best she could," Sam countered to Moore's last offering. The two deputies stared at the bar owner, mildly shocked. What was the matter with Sam? He had never been heard to defend anyone, regardless of the slander. Smith recovered from the remark first, and determined to forge ahead.

"Let's ask him if he saw anybody around here who looked like a bank robber, and get out of here," Smith said. Sam's heart raced, thinking what will Burk do when they come out the back door. Oddly, he thought, as Burk did earlier in the day, the wicked flee when no one pursues. If he ran, it could be bad for Burk and Sam.

"What the hell you have to bother my hired hand for? I'm sure he's going to quit as soon as he realizes no one works in this kind of heat. Then where do you think I'm going to get me another hand to dig that ditch out? Leave him alone. I can tell you he ain't seen nothing but the bottom of that ditch," Sam said, frowning at the two deputies, hoping he could send them back out the front door. He didn't want to take a chance on Burk's state of mind.

"Boy, he has dug himself quite a hole. Let's go, Ronnie. I really don't want to talk to ol' Joe now. My little brother and I used to follow him around. He was always good to us. Let's get out to the sale barn, see if they really do have any dogs that can find anything but a biscuit," Moore said. Smith looked at his partner, then at the bar owner, and shrugged. The two deputies exited the front door, leaving a relieved bar owner.

Sam could not know Burk decided he was not going to put up a fight if they came to arrest him. He promised himself, for whatever reason, be it fate, God, or something else, if he was not arrested, he was never going to allow himself to be put in this kind of position again. Steve Jones talked him into the cattle thievery, and Letha Mae talked him into this fiasco.

He vowed that, henceforth, he would walk his own path, regardless of where it took him, or the relationships lost. His mother was without self-discipline, and it cost her her life at an early age. She refused to tell him who his father was, and he could not look to that person to determine whether he could discipline himself. Regardless, Burk determined he was going to take charge of his life; let Letha Mae have the money, and fulfill her dream. It was not his dream.

"Joe Burk, you lucky son-of-a-bitch, get in here. The cops have gone. Where do you want to go?" Sam said, standing in the back door of the bar. He was grinning from ear to ear. Burk grinned back. His instinct that told him Sam was a friend panned out.

"I still need to make a call, Sam. Then, I'll know what I need to do," Burk said.

"Get on the phone, and get the call made. I don't trust that Smith. He's got too much sense to be a deputy."

Burk called Letha Mae. His face was wreathed in a smile as he turned back to Sam, and asked, "Sam, can you take me to Letha Mae James' house? It looks like this whole thing may work out, after all," he asserted in a chipper tone.

"I have no idea what you are talking about, and don't want to know. You have uncovered my sewer pipe enough so Joe Chapman can finish his plumbing job when it cools off later. That is all I hired you for when you walked up, and that's all I know about Joe Burk." Sam spouted the words as if he were testifying and threw a shirt to Burk.

"Put that on. I don't want you sweating on my seats in my car," Sam continued. He was more muscular than Burk, but the shirt wasn't a bad fit.

Sam said, "Do you know how to get to Paris by the farm to market roads? If you do, once you get to Paris, you should be all right. I don't think they'll expand their search until they run those dogs down trying to find you at the sale barn." Sam was referring to Paris, Texas, approximately seventy-five miles away.

Burk paused. Someone sooner or later was going to point out the dogs needed to be started on Main Street where the robbery took place. He didn't know how long his scent would linger in an area, or if the dogs would be unable to pick up his trail after he went into the creek. He estimated that he had waded in the creek for better than a mile. Also, he could not be sure no one saw him with Letha Mae at the church. He needed to be gone before any of these links came together. Burk and Sam got into the immaculate Cadillac, and left the bar, going to Letha Mae's.

THE CROW CHAMBER OF COMMERCE was revving up to really go all out in their Fourth of July celebration of the bicentennial in this year of 1976. The bicentennial quarters minted by the Federal Government were much in evidence, and an air of patriotism was pervasive in the community, and the entire country.

Don Wells, on his way to his quarter horses, reflected how few in the community remembered that, at this time last year, his loan company was being held up by two giant robbers. Wells still bore the scar on his forehead left by the pistol wielded by Burk, but it was more of a badge of honor than a scar. His heroics had erased much of the old rumor about his buying his way out of World War II. The local newspaper extolled his bravery in almost patriotic terms, and only Wells and Josie Williams, now Banks, knew the truth about the events that unfolded at the -Payday Loans.

His insurance company covered his loss, which was less than ten thousand dollars, and which he reported to the local newspaper as three thousand dollars; even at that much reduced figure, he was concerned that some copycat might be inspired to emulate the robbers. For people whose income always put them on the bottom rung of every statistic compiled, three thousand dollars was a sizable amount of money.

I miss Josie, he thought. When she received an envelope at Payday from Paris, Texas with no sender's name on it, she gasped at its contents, told him she needed to leave for a few minutes, and ran out. She returned less than thirty minutes later and told him she was marrying Dennis Banks, and moving to Mount Pleasant, Texas.

Wells knew that Dennis Banks, the young loan officer was being courted by his former employee, and he was planning to move back to Mount Pleasant. His understanding, however, concerning Josie, was she refused to move with him. Whatever was in the envelope caused her to change her mind, he suspected.

Sylvia left him, too, enrolling at the University of Oklahoma, taking advantage of Title IX, and going to play basketball. His daughter told him the new female coach at OU had the reputation of liking other females more than Wells considered normal, and Wells wondered anew about Sylvia. Was her child a way to quiet speculation about her sexual preferences? Regardless, Wells was almost relieved about Sylvia leaving, although he was concerned about replacing her in terms of the black community. He felt she acted rashly when she attacked the smaller robber instead of activating the alarm near her hiding place in the rear.

She responded to his query by stating she felt that she could handle the robbers better than any of Crow's police force. Her attitude was defiant. Wells was glad he didn't have to make any further decisions about her. The black business she brought in stayed with him even after her departure.

Wells replaced both women with two other single mothers who needed to work, but he knew that he had lost the best team he ever had.

Steven Parker

CHAPTER

15

SAM STONE SURPRISED the Saturday night crowd by stopping the activities and reading an article in the Paris, Texas, newspaper about Joe Burk. Some wondered what happened to Burk, but did not concern themselves over it much. Stone gathered three of Burk's running buddies around him, and read the article to them. The article gushed about a thirty-year-old, married ex-convict with two children enrolling at Paris Junior College and becoming a "walk-on" for the basketball team. Now on scholarship, he was the starting point guard. There was a picture of Burk with his wife, and children. The junior college coach was standing in the background. The human interest feature also stated the former convict was working part-time as youth director at a local Baptist church, aided in this endeavor by his wife's mentally challenged brother, Luther.

"Hey, that wife's Letha Mae James. I wondered what happened to her," one of the onlookers stated. "Boy, I was sorry to see her go. Reckon I ought to go over to Paris and see if ol' Joe needs help with his homework?"

"Shit, Bob, you couldn't handle it even if she let you in the door. Do you guys recognize the coach? That's Gary Jiles who used to play for Hayward. He and Burk used to play against each other, and, as I recall, Burk used to eat his lunch. Hell, Jiles was not surprised by Burk's play, I don't care how old ole Joe is," Moses Wills contributed.

The year before, Burk, Letha Mae, Bugger and the two boys had, indeed, traversed the farm to market roads to Paris. The circuitous route was unnecessary because the main roads to Paris were not being checked. Upon arriving in the Texas town, Burk pulled into a small restaurant for a restroom and drink break. He determined during the drive that he was not going to Mexico, and hoped he was not going to be a fugitive. Still, he was saddened by having to break this news to Letha Mae. What she said to him in the church parking lot before he began his trek into the creek bothered him. He knew she was sincere, and also knew his feelings for her was as close to "love" as he would ever get; he knew that he loved her, whatever "that" was. But, he also knew they or he could have no real kind of life in Mexico.

To keep from talking to her immediately, he picked up the local newspaper and scanned the sports pages. The picture of Gary Jiles, his former basketball competitor from Hayward, drew his attention. Jiles was going to take over the basketball job at the junior college after a surprise resignation from the head coach.

"What an opportunity for Jiles," thought Burk. Then, raising his eyebrows, he thought, *What an opportunity for me. This guy knows me, knows I can play basketball. I'll see him, talk him into giving me a chance; I won't squander this chance.* Would his former opponent be willing to take a chance on him? Would the coach's superiors allow him to take a chance?

Letha Mae noted the raised eyebrows and asked, "Joe, what is it? What are you thinking?" Something seemed different about Joe all the way to Paris. She thought, *He kept looking at me as if he wanted to say something, but could not. Maybe I shouldn't have told him I loved him, but I don't care. I do, and I'm not going to give him up without a fight— not even if he wants to go.*

"Letha Mae, I'm not going to Mexico. I'm not a Mexican, and don't want to be, not even a rich one. I'm not going to make any claim on the money. You can have it. I do want to keep this money I have in my pocket, just enough to get by on for a little while," Burk said, looking at the table so he would not have to see her expression. Letha Mae's heart sank. What was Joe going to do? It was as if he heard her question.

Burk continued, "Do you see this guy? I played basketball against him. I know him. He and I were friends. I believe he will let me play for him. I'm going to try. If he doesn't, I'll go somewhere else. I know I can play. I just need a chance. I'm going to play, then I'm going to coach. I am not going to Mexico," Burk said, setting his jaw. He didn't want to argue, but he had made his decision, and he was not going to change it.

Letha Mae knew argument was futile. Still, he had not addressed their relationship, and she had to know even if the news was something she did not want to hear.

"Joe, I want you to have whatever you want, and I'll fight to help you get it. But what about us? If you have to play basketball, can't we help you? I love you. Do you love me?" Letha Mae said, attempting to control her desperation. The money and Mexico seemed meaningless at this point and Burk did not hesitate before answering. His voice was confident.

"Yes, Letha Mae, I love you. Probably too much. But, if you stay with me, we can't spend that money. I'm going to have to report to my parole officer, and get this arrangement okay'ed by him. I don't think it will be a problem, but who knows. If he does say I can do it, I can't be spending a lot of money without arousing suspicion. It wouldn't be fair to you, or the kids. I know how much you counted on this thing coming through, and now it looks like we pulled it off. I just don't want it," Burk said.

"Then I don't want it. I just want to be with you," Letha Mae said.

Bugger and the two boys were listening to the whole conversation, going from one talker to the other like a tennis match. Now, Bugger determined it was his turn to speak.

"I want to give my share to Josie. She deserves it," Bugger said. Letha Mae and Burk looked at each other. Neither wanted to address Bugger's desire.

Letha Mae said, "Let's talk about Josie later, and decide what we are going to do about all of us right now. Are we going to split up or stay together? Joe, it's your decision."

Letha Mae looked out the window and Burk thought she was going to start crying.

"We can make it work, Letha Mae, but it will mean you will have to go back to waitressing. I may be able to get some part-time work if it doesn't violate some rule. You can have Bugger's check transferred here—but not for happy tobaccy. The money? I want you to deposit it somewhere I can't touch it. Then, we can have it for emergencies, or you can split any time you want without being broke." Burk then thought to himself, *"What a fool I am."*

Letha Mae's survivor instinct took over. She liked the idea of having control over a large sum of money. Having it to fall back on meant she could be more independent at any job. She would not have to flirt to make tips, and grabby hands could be slapped if you were not afraid of losing your job. But she was not finished.

"Joe, if we're going to do this thing, we're going to get married. I am not going to wait tables while my man plays basketball unless I am married to him." Letha Mae looked at Burk almost defiantly.

"Dammit, Letha Mae, don't you think I ought to be the one who does the proposing. What are you teaching these boys?" Burk questioned her sternly, but she noticed the twinkle in his eyes, and after he looked at the boys, she noticed both of them were grinning. He took her hands and looked into her eyes. "Letha Mae James, will you marry me?" Burk queried, smiling at his bride-to-be.

She kissed him long and hard. The boys and Bugger looked at each other, and at the kissing couple. The other diners munched on their burgers and fries, some thinking those folks ought to rent a room.

Steven Parker

CHAPTER

16

DEPUTY SMITH STOPPED BY to see Sam Stone a week after the robbery. He told Sam the state dogs used for man-hunting were given the option of going to Tulsa to track an escaped convict there, or coming to Crow to track their bandit. The dog owner opted for Tulsa. Smith opined it was because the dog owner could get television coverage from the Tulsa stations, whereas there would have been no television coverage from Crow. Little Dixie television viewers got their news from Shreveport, and Texarkana, and it was unlikely those television stations were going to send anyone to Southeastern Oklahoma to cover a loan company robber's trackdown. Some effort was made to interest local coon hound owners and other dog men in putting their dogs on the scent, but the only taker of the offer suffered an embarrassment which kept the local wags talking for days. The coon hunter's lead dog known as ol' Blue broke from the pack after being unloaded, and headed in a beeline for an attractive female dispatcher who was busily flirting with an out-of-town highway patrolman, and did not see the dog approaching. Ol' Blue stuck his nose in her crotch, which immediately got her attention.

The crowd of law enforcers and concerned citizens began heehawing as the embarrassed woman backed up, and ol' Blue followed her. It was too much for the dispatcher. She cracked ol' Blue on his active nose with her clipboard, sending him howling to his owner. There were some ribald comments about ol' Blue having his priorities straight, and several joking offers to buy the dog. The owner glared at the woman and the laughing onlookers, and led his dog away, ignoring the pleas of the sheriff. The manhunt via dog sniffing was over.

No useful fingerprints were found in the 1957 Ford, nor anything else of consequence. Bugger's discarded scarf and hat were found, but the fingerprints did not match any prints on file. The one observer who was willing to come forward and discuss Bugger's headlong flight described him as five inches taller, and fifty pounds heavier than he was.

The other descriptions of the bandits varied. Wells remembered both as being more than six feet tall, and weighing more than 200 pounds. Sylvia Murdock stated the robber she put on the ground could not have been more than five feet, eight inches tall, and did not weigh more than one hundred and fifty pounds. Josie, who grappled with the small robber, agreed with Sylvia about the height, but thought he was about twenty pounds heavier. The pickup owner who was going to shoot Burk said he was at least six feet tall, and weighed more than two hundred pounds. The bulky jackets had served their purpose.

The descriptions of the gun were not any more exact. It was described as nickel plated, or blue steel; a 357 Magnum, or a .45 calibre.

Smith told Sam that Josie underwent heavy grilling about the robbery being an inside job because the small robber called her the large robber's girlfriend. She was also quizzed heavily about the money found in her bra at the hospital where she was taken for treatment for her knees and elbows. Wells and the teller at the bank confirmed the packets did come from the bank. Josie stuck to her story that she had been saving the money, and put it in her safety deposit box at the bank. The deputy confirmed she visited her safety deposit box at the bank that day. Her marriage to Dennis Banks and removal to Texas caused him some consternation, but he had nothing on which he could hold her.

Josie realized before the grilling that one of the robbers was Bugger. She could not come up with any reason, though, why she should tell the authorities, particularly when she determined her negotiations with him might be much more fruitful—if she could find him. If she told them, and they found him, she got nothing but a warm thank you, and a handshake. It was not enough for Josie Williams, not by a long shot. Particularly not after she heard that Rennie Morton died.

The ninety-three year old woman died a week after she had been robbed, although she was unaware of being fleeced. The medical examiner wrote she died of myocardial infarction, which meant he had no idea why she died. The old woman who had shown so much heart at the casinos in Las Vegas, that two of her favorite gambling places held a moment of silence in her honor. One niece who knew of the old gambler's habit of storing large sums of cash threatened to sue the bank, but, as the inventory of the safety deposit box revealed abstracts of property, deeds, stocks, and bonds—items usually found in a safety deposit box— her lawyer convinced her it was unlikely the bank could be held liable for missing cash, which was not supposed to be hidden in the lock box—if it ever existed.

Josie was not surprised to receive the envelope from Paris, Texas, which included a cashier's check made payable to her. The purchaser of the check was Luther James. Although Josie hoped for more, she decided to take it, and begin a new life in Mt. Pleasant, Texas, with her new husband. She reasoned also that now she knew where Bugger was, more payments could be forthcoming. She would wait and see.

Shortly after the robbery, Sam Stone had a visit from Ronnie Smith, the deputy sheriff now nicknamed "Bluebird" by some of Sam's patrons after he told them about the deputy's proficiency with the English language. The deputy had no idea why he got this nickname, and only the former alumni of Miss Haskins' first grade reading class were fully aware of the significance. Sam suspected Deputy Smith was not there to simply enlighten him on the progress, or lack thereof, of the case. Smith came to the point. Burk had not been seen at the Hoot and Holler Club the night before the robbery, and had not been seen in the brawl with the Dierks boys. Lightnin' Bob was seriously injured, but no one saw Burk. Sam knew Lightnin' Bob, a Choctaw Indian who was a good fighter when he wasn't drunk, but a punching bag when he was, which was more and more often. He was not surprised to hear Lightnin' Bob was not expected to live. He guessed the deputy wasn't able to talk to Lightnin' Bob, or he would not be here.

"I never told you Burk was in the brawl with the Dierks boys. I assumed he was after I saw his face. I knew there was a fight over at the Hoot and Holler, and I know the ol' boy who owns the place doesn't stop fights, even if they end in killings. Look at Lightnin' Bob. I'd bet two-to-one he was drunk, and that guy didn't stop it. Not many people will miss him, but I don't aim to see anybody get killed here, I don't care how sorry people think he is," Sam said, letting the lawman know he controlled the events around his bar.

"If he didn't get the messed up face at the Hoot and Holler, where did he get it?" Smith asked, not going to be put off by the bar owner's change of direction.

"Hell, knowing Burk, he could have gotten it at the No Name, the Silver Bullet, the Black Hat, or any bar in the county where someone was willing to fight him. I didn't quiz him about his face. Why don't you ask him?"

"His parole officer said he's getting ready to go to junior college in Paris, and he's not interested in bringing him here. I don't want to go to Texas unless I have to, and the sheriff thinks it's a wild goose chase. He also said he didn't want to cause any more trouble for a boy who thinks he is an orphan, but isn't. Told me to ask you about that." Smith noted a slight tightening of the bar owner's eyes, but he received no response.

"What is it with this guy Burk? Trace wouldn't even come out here with me today. Why does everyone seem to be protecting him?" Smith asked after Stone didn't respond. The deputy was preparing to launch into a discourse about law and order when Sam began talking.

"Smith, you're a smart boy. Smarter than they usually hire around here. Don't you think you ought to respect what the sheriff says? He's getting older, and apparently gabbier than he used to be. He's going to be looking around for someone to take his place. Could be you. Besides, if Burk were involved, do you really think he would really run only seventy-five miles, and then call his parole officer?" Sam said, using a persuasive voice to guide the deputy away from Burk.

"You're probably right. If he does step down, and I run for his job, will you support me, Sam?" the deputy asked, determining he was not going to receive any aid in his investigation from this quarter.

"Boy, if I came out in public for you, it would be the kiss of death. But I'll do what I can for you," Sam promised. The deputy left, pondering about whether to cross his boss, and Sam Stone, and go to Paris, Texas, or let the matter die. The matter died.

Burk's former companions at Sam's Drive-In and Bar then looked at Sam, and the newspaper photograph. "Who would have ever thought Burk would be a Baptist youth director? I'd believe it more if the story was that Letha Mae fucked the preacher, and Burk beat him up. When he comes back, I'm going to ride the hell out of him," Moses said.

"I pray to God he never comes back," Sam said, looking at the trio who knew Burk all his life. They stood silently, not knowing what to say. What was the matter with Sam, anyway? First, cutting a newspaper story out of an out of town newspaper about a guy who they all liked, but would not have missed if no one ever told them what happened to him. And now, praying to God he never came back. Sam picked up his newspaper story, and went back behind the bar. The matter was closed forever at Sam's Bar and Drive-In.

Steven Parker

Acknowledgements

While this narrative was written as I practiced law in Tecumseh, Oklahoma, publishing this novel was the result of many talented people coming together to transform the manuscript into an actual book. Specifically, I want to thank Amy Susan Wilson, Publisher of Red Dirt Press, for her encouragement and insight regarding the direction in which to take this manuscript. I also want to thank Laura Smyth for her work on the cover design, interior, and for her skill as an editor. Additionally, a heartfelt thanks to Amanda Rosamond, a talented photographer who managed to capture just the right light, setting; additionally, a thank you is in order to William "Bill" Bernhardt for his insight and advice on issues related to publication of this novel. I am so glad I have this opportunity to thank each of you publicly.

—*Steven L. Parker*

www.ingramcontent.com/pod-product-compliance
Lightning Source LLC
Chambersburg PA
CBHW070549180626
46817CB00005B/1751